# FLIGHT 29 DOWN

# Survival

Stan Rogow Productions · Grosset & Dunlap

GROSSET & DUNLAP
Published by the Penguin Group
Penguin Group (USA) Inc., 375 Hudson Street, New York, New York 10014, U.S.A.
Penguin Group (Canada), 90 Eglinton Avenue East, Suite 700, Toronto, Ontario,
Canada M4P 2Y3
(a division of Pearson Penguin Canada Inc.)
Penguin Books Ltd, 80 Strand, London WC2R 0RL, England
Penguin Ireland, 25 St Stephen's Green, Dublin 2, Ireland
(a division of Penguin Books Ltd)
Penguin Group (Australia), 250 Camberwell Road, Camberwell, Victoria 3124, Australia
(a division of Pearson Australia Group Pty Ltd)
Penguin Books India Pvt Ltd, 11 Community Centre, Panchsheel Park,
New Delhi - 110 017, India
Penguin Group (NZ), 67 Apollo Drive, Mairangi Bay, Auckland 1311, New Zealand
(a division of Pearson New Zealand Ltd)
Penguin Books (South Africa) (Pty) Ltd, 24 Sturdee Avenue, Rosebank,
Johannesburg 2196, South Africa

Penguin Books Ltd, Registered Offices:
80 Strand, London WC2R 0RL, England

Published by Grosset & Dunlap, a division of Penguin Young Readers Group,
345 Hudson Street, New York, New York 10014. GROSSET & DUNLAP is a trademark
of Penguin Group (USA) Inc. Printed in the U.S.A.

Library of Congress Cataloging-in-Publication Data

Sorrells, Walter.
Survival / by Walter Sorrells.
p. cm. -- (Flight 29 down ; #7)
"Based on the teleplays by D.J. MacHale."
"Based on the TV series created by D.J. MacHale."
"Stan Rogow."
ISBN 978-0-448-44432-1 (pbk.)
I. MacHale, D. J. II. Rogow, Stan. III. Stan Rogow Productions. IV. Flight 29 down (Television
program) V. Title.
PZ7.S7216Sur 2007
[Fic]--dc22
2006100775

ISBN 978-0-448-44432-1                    10 9 8 7 6 5 4 3 2 1

# Survival

**A novelization by**
**Walter Sorrells**

**Adapted from the**
**teleplays by D.J. MacHale**
**Based on the**
**TV series created by**
**D.J. MacHale**
**Stan Rogow**

Stan Rogow Productions · Grosset & Dunlap

# PROLOGUE

## DAY NINE ON THE ISLAND

**N**athan walked out of the boys' tent and stretched. It was another beautiful day on the island. In front of him lay the long white beach where he and his friends had crash-landed just a little over a week earlier.

He kept thinking he'd wake up one day lying in his own bed, and this would all turn out to be a dream.

He sighed. Another day stuck on this island "paradise."

As he started walking over toward the other tent where the water was stored, he noticed a girl's necklace lying on a chair they'd pulled out of the wreck of flight 29 DWN. It was a delicate silver chain with coral and amythyst beads. Didn't

Abby Fujimoto wear a necklace like that?

Next to the necklace was a book with the word JOURNAL printed on the front in neat black letters. It seemed to have been intentionally left where everybody would see it.

As he picked up the necklace to examine it more closely, Nathan heard someone else approaching. He looked up and saw Daley coming toward him, yawning and raking her fingers through her wavy red hair.

"Where's Abby?" Nathan said.

"She's sleeping," Daley said.

"No, she's not," Melissa said, emerging from the girls' tent.

Nathan picked up the journal and noticed a piece of paper tucked between the pages. It read, "Read this."

"Hey, look," he said. "She left us a note."

Taylor popped out of the tent. Unlike everybody else—who looked like they had just woken up—Taylor's hair somehow managed to look perfect. "Hey!" she said. "Where's my backpack? My eyeliner is in there."

Nathan opened the journal and started reading aloud. It was Abby's graceful handwriting. "'Please forgive me,'" he read. "'This is something I have to do. Jackson, I believe you; it's about right here, right now. And right now I've got to find the others.'"

Nathan was stunned. Abby had left the camp

on the first day with the pilot, Captain Russell, and two other kids from the Hartwell School, Ian and Jory. She had gotten separated from them, then fought her way back to camp. Why would she leave again? After all that she'd gone through out there in the woods, you'd think she would have wanted to stay with the group.

"She took my backpack?" Taylor said. "I can't believe she took my eyeliner. This is a *disaster*!"

Nathan kept reading. " 'Please don't follow me. I'll be fine. I know you'll understand because you'd do the same if one of you were lost. I'm going to find Captain Russell and the others, and I'm going to bring them back, I promise. Try not to worry. Make more happy memories. Love, Abby.' "

Nathan looked up at his friends. "We have to go after her!"

Jackson shook his head. "No, we don't."

Sometimes Nathan just didn't get Jackson. It was obvious that Abby was going to be in a lot more danger if she was out there by herself in the jungle than if she were here with everybody else. Ian and Jory were with Captain Russell. He was a grown-up. He'd take care of them. Why did she want to risk her neck for no reason?

"What if she gets lost again?" Nathan said to Jackson.

Jackson spread his hands. "What are we gonna do, Nathan? Drag her back? Tie her to a tree? If she wants to go, she'll just go again."

Melissa frowned thoughtfully. "Maybe we could help her find the others!" she said.

"Yeah," Eric said sarcastically. "Then maybe we could get ourselves lost, too."

Taylor looked around the group. "So what do we do?"

The youngest member of the group, Daley's little brother Lex, piped up. "She knows the island," he said matter-of-factly. "She'll come back. Eventually."

"Hopefully they'll all come back," Daley said.

Nathan shook his head. He didn't like it. All this lone hero stuff got people in trouble. It had been nine days since Captain Russell and the others had left. Only Abby had come back. The island wasn't *that* big. He was afraid something bad had happened to them. No, sticking together and hunkering down until they got rescued—that was their only hope.

But Abby was gone now. The truth was, there wasn't much they could do for her now.

Jackson looked off toward the trees. "Good luck, Abby," he said softly.

# ONE

**TWO WEEKS LATER: THE PRESENT**

## Eric

Dude, I am *sick* of this! It's been, like, three weeks now.

When do we start giving up hope of rescue? A week? A month? Hey, come on, we're fooling ourselves if we think every boat in the Pacific Ocean is looking for us anymore. I bet it was probably a big deal at first. Kids disappear into the ocean, blah blah blah—I'm sure all the news channels were talking about nothing else . . . for about ten minutes.

But then something else happened. Some famous actor got arrested for acting weird at the mall or something—and, boom, we're yesterday's news.

"Oh, yeah, those kids on the plane? Did anybody ever find them? I can't remember."

Nobody cares anymore. Except maybe our parents. And what can they do? Even Taylor's dad, who's, like, one of the richest guys in California. What's he gonna do—hire every airplane in the world to search the entire Pacific Ocean? Don't think so.

I think we're kidding ourselves with this whole sit-around-and-wait routine. It's time to stop dreaming and start thinking up a way to get out of here.

After he switched off the video camera, Eric felt a little deflated. It was all well and good to say he wanted to do something about getting rescued. But . . . like what?

It wasn't like he was an airplane mechanic. And they didn't exactly have a boat handy.

He set the camera down by the shelter they'd built a few days back and walked disconsolately along the shoreline. Off in the distance, everybody was all busy and cheerful looking. Daley and Nathan were doing their busy-bee routine, working on some kind of little helpful project. Melissa was cooking. Lex was carrying a handful of fruit out of the forest. Eric could hear the sound of Jackson's machete hacking away back in the trees. Jackson had been sick as a dog with this stomach bug called giardia only a couple of days ago, but he was still trying to pitch in. Even Taylor was down at the far end of the beach fishing.

Eric kept walking glumly, kicking the sand as he went.

Then he spotted something washing up on the shore. A scrap of wood. It wasn't just some tree that had fallen in the ocean. It was lumber, a board. Man-made.

He grabbed it and picked it up. There was some writing on it.

*Whoa!* he thought as he read the script inked onto the side of the wood. An idea started forming in his mind.

Maybe this was the answer to their problems!

He began to run back toward the camp. "Hey!" he called. "Hey! Guys!"

"How many did you get?" Daley said as Taylor walked back into camp. Taylor was carrying a stick with some silvery fish skewered on it.

Taylor held up the stick. "Only two. It seems like we've caught most of the good ones in that shallow area down there. We may need to start fishing farther down the beach."

Daley sighed loudly. It was a recurring theme. They seemed to have gathered most of the food within a reasonable distance of their camp. They were having to travel farther and farther distances every day to find anything edible.

"Hey!" a voice called. "Check this out!"

Eric burst into the camp waving . . . well, it looked like a piece of wood.

"Wow!" Taylor said. "A piece of slimy, gross-looking old board. How fascinating."

Eric didn't seem to be bothered by Taylor. "Look." He tapped his finger on the wood. Daley could see that something was printed on the board. "Right here!"

Nathan leaned toward it and squinted at the board. "'Marianas Shipping. Agana Harbor. Guh.'" He looked up. "Guh? What's guh?"

"Not *guh*." Eric kept waving the board excitedly. "G-U. See where the board's broken? If it wasn't broken, it would say G-U-A-M. Guam!"

Taylor looked around blankly. "Clueless," she said.

Lex joined them from the path and said, "It probably floated here on the current."

"Exactly! Extra bonus for Boy Brainiac." Eric clapped Lex on the shoulder. "I've always said we should listen to this kid more often."

"No, you haven't," Taylor said. "Usually you say he's an annoying—"

Eric waved his hands, cutting her off. "Never

mind that. Point is, if this thing made it all the way from Guam, then there's a serious current going past the island."

Daley was not following him. Obviously, there were currents in the ocean. That was hardly big news. "So what?" she said.

"Hello!" Eric stared at her like she was a moron. "Currents don't stop. They keep on . . . currenting. If it can carry a piece of wood this far, it might carry something bigger."

Nathan scratched his head. "Like . . . a really big piece of waterlogged junk?"

"Come on! Like . . . a *raft*. With us on it."

Daley scoffed. Eric was always looking for a magic bullet. Instead of doing sensible, normal hard work. Like cooking. Or gathering food. Or tending the fire, or—

"You're kidding, right?" Nathan said, anticipating Daley's next words.

"Hmm . . ." said Melissa. "Gee, that sounds kind of ambitious."

"A raft?" Taylor said. "Like, in the water?"

"Not gonna happen, Eric," Daley added.

"Why not?" Eric said.

There was a moment of silence. Finally Nathan said, "Uh, there's a whole bunch of answers to that. Starting with certain death, right up there on the tippy-top of the list."

Eric's face was starting to get red. "We gotta face reality, people. It's been three weeks."

"And one day," Lex added.

"Yeah, okay, three weeks and one day," Eric pushed on. "Whatever. What I'm saying is, if they were looking for us anywhere near here, we'd all be home sitting at the pool and sipping ice cold sodas. Best case scenario, they're looking in the wrong place. Worst case? Hey, our parents have all had memorial services for us and they're getting on with their lives. Face it, at some point, they're just gonna stop looking."

"Don't even think that!" Daley said. She was sick of Eric always undermining everybody's morale.

Eric's usually cocky expression faded. His voice grew quieter. "Guys, I want to keep hoping as much as anybody. Believe me, I do! But when do we start taking control of our lives?"

There was a brief silence.

"So you're really being serious?" Melissa said finally. "You really want to build a raft and float off into . . . whatever's out there?"

Eric cleared his throat. "Well, no. Not yet, anyway. I think we should build a small raft—for two people maybe. Just to see if we can do it. That way we can test the current."

"Test for what?" Daley said skeptically. Eric was always coming up with plans—but they were never practical.

"For direction," Lex said.

"Exactly!" Eric put up his hand as though to high-five Lex.

Lex didn't seem to see Eric's hand, though. Daley could tell that his mind was already working on the problem. Once that happened, Lex tended to lose awareness of his surroundings. "We flew west from Guam toward Palau," Lex said. "If that chunk of wood floated here on a western current, it might keep on going to Asia."

He picked up a stick and immediately started drawing something on the sand. A map, Daley assumed.

"And if it's an eastern current?" she said.

Nathan looked down at the map Lex was drawing. "If it goes east . . ." He pointed at the map. "If it goes east, it'll just dump smack into the middle of the Pacific."

Everyone looked glum. Which was okay with Daley. She didn't think this was such a hot idea, anyway.

"I'm only saying we do a test," Eric said. "Who knows? If we're stuck here for another couple of months, we might start getting desperate. At least we'd have a backup plan."

"I don't think we'd ever get that desperate," Daley said.

Eric looked her in the eye. "Fine. That's your opinion. Let's put it to a vote. Who's in favor of building a raft to test the currents?"

Eric raised his arm sharply in the air.

Daley looked around, expecting to see a solid show of disapproval. To her shock, Jackson, Lex, and Taylor slowly lifted their hands. She couldn't believe it! Every minute they invested in some nutty scheme like this was a minute that couldn't be spent fishing or gathering fruit or cleaning clothes or boiling safe drinking water.

"Seriously?" she said. "With all the important stuff we have to do around here? That's what you guys really want?"

Jackson shrugged.

Eric smiled smugly. "Four to three, baby. Four to three."

Daley looked at him sourly. "Fair enough," she said. "Four to three. We build a raft." She paused and looked around the group. "I just hope we're not making a huge mistake."

## Daley

Democracy. That's what we agreed to.

But it makes me wonder how smart a democracy can be when the majority votes to do something so totally idiotic!

Okay, let's go with the idea. Let's say the current's going in the right direction. What then? We don't know a thing about how to make a boat that would hold up in a big storm. We've had three major storms since we've been here. We'd be pretty much guaranteed of getting hit with a big storm before we got to wherever we were going. The waves here are humongous. They'd tear a *real* boat apart. Much less a bunch of moldy old stuff held together with string and bubble gum.

And do we have any clue as to where we'd be going? Zero. We know squat about navigation. We have no motor. We don't even have sails. And even if we did, how do you even steer a raft?

And what about food? We have no way of storing food. Even if we could find enough extra food that we could spend weeks drying fruit and smoking fish . . . what then? We might be floating around out there for months. And then there's drinking water. No way in the world do we have enough room to store drinking water for a month or two.

It's crazy. It's just plain nuts!

# Two

**E**ric watched as the other kids dragged a variety of building material up to the shelter and dumped them in the weedy sand. Mostly they'd been cutting bamboo. But some of them had gathered vines and fallen tree branches out of the jungle. It was kind of fun watching everybody else slave away on *his* project. Not that he hadn't been working hard, too. Things sure were easier to do when you felt motivated!

"Whew!" Nathan said, staggering up to the pile and dumping a huge armload of bamboo onto it. "Tell me this is enough."

Eric smiled. "Perfect!" he said.

Nathan looked at the pile and shook his head. "I don't even know where to start," he said.

"Ah, but *I* do," Eric said triumphantly. "I've

been thinking about making a raft for weeks. It's all in my head and dying to come out."

"Now there's a scary thought," Daley said.

Everybody else had been participating reasonably cheerfully. But Daley had been sniping the whole time. If it had been her idea, man, she'd have been driving everybody crazy trying to get them to work harder. But since it was Eric's stroke of genius, naturally she couldn't get with the program.

"All we have to do is make my idea real," Eric said, feeling a swell of pride in his chest. "Listen up, here's what we're gonna do . . ."

The group worked all afternoon. Eric had been planning the boat for weeks, but he hadn't actually done any experiments, so a certain amount of adjustment in the plan was required. The basic idea was simple enough, though. Bundles of bamboo were lashed together in groups of six or seven. Then those groups were lashed together, with a few flotation devices from the plane added for support. Then branches from the forest would be lashed crossways to offer extra support.

Eric was kind of amazed at how well everything went. As the raft began to grow, he pictured himself floating on the ocean, bobbing along on the current as a pleasant breeze blew over him.

Once the current took over, there'd be nothing to do but kick back and enjoy the ride. He imagined a mango juice drink in his hand, a tiny paper umbrella sticking out of the top . . .

Okay, maybe that was going a little overboard. But seriously, how long could it take to hit land somewhere else? A couple or three days?

No problem. He'd pack plenty of dried fish, plenty of water. Then when he hit land, everybody would be totally amazed! They'd drive him to the American Embassy, and then people would be cheering for him and calling him a hero. He'd probably be on TV!

Man, wouldn't Taylor be envious?

"Eric! Helloooo! Earth to Eric!"

A voice cut through Eric's daydream.

"Sorry, what?" he said.

Daley was staring at him. "What do you think?" she said. "Are we done?"

Eric drew himself up, put a serious look on his face, and walked slowly around the raft. It was about six feet long and eight feet wide. Plenty long for a test. The *real* raft would be bigger. Maybe fifteen by fifteen?

He reached out, grabbed a vine, and yanked on it. It held. He poked and prodded and shook various parts of the vessel.

"That's what *I'm* talking about," he said with a smile when he was done. He figured he needed to act like he wasn't completely satisfied, though, so he added, "Just a couple of finishing touches and we'll be good to go. First thing in the morning, I'm floating away." He looked around, realizing he hadn't even thought about food since this morning. He was *starving*! "What's for dinner, guys?"

Melissa had brought a basket of fruit, so he plopped down and started wolfing down a mango.

"Nice work, team!" he added. He groaned with pleasure. "You know what I'm gonna do when I hit civilization? Eat a pizza, watch a movie, and sleep in a real bed."

He grinned and looked around at the circle of faces. As he munched on the mango, he was conscious of an odd silence. Everybody seemed to be looking at him apprehensively.

Melissa and Nathan glanced at each other, like they were about to give him some kind of bad news. *Oh no,* Eric thought. *What now?*

"Look, Eric," Nathan said. "We don't know if this raft is a good idea or not. But one thing's for certain . . . you can't go."

Eric felt a burst of anger. "What!" He hopped up off the sand. "No way! We voted. Majority rules, dude. You can't back out now."

Daley spoke next. "This isn't about the raft, Eric. It's about who's going to sail it."

What was she babbling about? He was so sick of people trying to mess with his ideas. "What do you mean—*who's going to sail it*? I am. It was my idea, I'm going. You guys fight over shotgun."

Melissa looked at him with concern. "Eric, I'm not saying this to be mean, but ... you're a terrible swimmer. Remember in gym back in ninth grade how—"

"Whoa, whoa, whoa!" Eric interrupted. Eric didn't want to think about that. There had been this swimming test and he'd almost drowned. It was one of those tests where you had to jump in fully clothed, then pull your pants off and use them as a flotation device. He'd gotten tangled in his pants, and Coach Morganthau ended up having to drag him out of the pool. "That was a long time ago. Anyway, there's no swimming involved. It's a raft. You sit on the raft. The raft does all the floating for you."

"And what if something happens?" Melissa said. "What if the raft sinks?"

"If that raft goes down," Daley added, "you'll go down, too. Probably with whoever is with you."

Taylor nodded. "They're right, Eric. You're not the strongest swimmer."

"I don't care!" Eric felt a flush coming into his cheeks. "It's my choice."

Daley looked around at the group. "We could put this to a vote."

Eric felt cornered. He'd been so fixated on his dream of getting out of there, so consumed with designing the raft, that it hadn't really occurred to him the thing might not work. But now that it was actually built . . . well, it looked pretty sturdy. But it wouldn't be too cool if the thing sank out there. He really *would* be in trouble. "All right," Eric said. "At least while we test it out, I guess I'm willing to let somebody else go. As long as *somebody* goes."

"Who's it gonna be?" Taylor said.

"Melissa and Taylor aren't real strong swimmers, either," Nathan said. "Lex is just a kid. And Jackson's still a little weak from that stomach bug that he had the other day. So that leaves . . ."

Eric suddenly felt peeved. "You and Daley? No. No way!" Typical, typical, typical. First they told you your idea was stupid. Then when it turned out that it worked, they did everything they could to hog all the glory. "You guys don't even think it's a good idea!"

"It doesn't matter what we think. Majority rules so . . . we go."

Eric felt like arguing. But what was the point? Lately Nathan and Daley had gotten to be like two heads on one body. Whenever one of them said anything, the other one agreed. And since they were little Mr. and Miss Leadership, once they decided on something, they almost always got their way. When they'd first come to the island, all they did was fight. But now? The way they looked at each other? The way they were all "Oh-Nathan-you're-so-smart," "Oh-yeah-Daley-you-have-such-brilliant-judgment"—it was totally obvious they had the hots for each other.

It was gross just being around them. And extremely irritating.

"Forget it," Eric said. "Do whatever you want. I'll finish the raft. Just leave me alone, okay?"

Nathan and Daley walked silently down to the edge of the beach and looked out at the ocean. Nathan threw a small piece of wood into the water. It moved swiftly along the shoreline.

"I think Eric's right. I think the water's flowing west. Pretty fast, too."

Daley nodded, but didn't speak. She'd been feeling nervous around Nathan for . . . well, ever since she'd slid down that ravine and he'd come and saved her. They seemed to be getting closer and closer. Like . . . *really* close. She'd finally had to tell him a couple of days ago that getting involved with each other here was a really bad idea. But every time she looked at him, she had this really great feeling and—

"Scared?" Nathan asked.

"A little," she said. There was a brief silence. "About a lot of things."

"Don't worry," Nathan said confidently. "At the first sign of trouble, we'll head back in."

"It's not just the raft," Daley said, feeling a hum of anxiety in her chest. "I'm, uh . . . to be honest, I'm starting to second guess myself."

"You? That's a first."

It was the sort of comment that would have driven her bananas just a few weeks ago. But now? She threw him a look. But the truth was, she didn't feel mad at all.

"Sorry," Nathan said. "Cheap shot. What's the problem?"

Daley hesitated. Why was it so hard talking about your feelings? Instead of saying what she really meant, she dodged the issue. "Floating to civilization is romantic, but totally unrealistic. It makes me think that as much as we want a democracy, the majority doesn't always make the right decision."

Nathan nodded. "Sure, it's messy. But it's the best system we've got."

"Is it?"

"I think so," Nathan said. "And we agreed to it. So that means whether we like it or not, tomorrow morning you and I are floating out to sea."

"Have you ever . . . have you ever felt like a current was sucking you along," she said, "sucking you along faster than you can swim? And so you're gonna end up someplace that you didn't want to go?"

Nathan shrugged. "Nah, I mostly swim at the pool."

Which wasn't really what Daley was talking about at all. And Nathan knew it. But if he didn't want to talk about it . . . Daley sighed and stared out at the water. The sun was coming down over the Pacific now, glinting on the waves. They were gentle here on the shore. But in the distance she could see the big rollers coming in off the ocean, breaking on the sandbar way out in the water. You couldn't actually see the sandbar. But you knew it was there because the really big waves broke on it. Daley knew that if they drifted out past the sandbar, they'd end up in the big waves. And, boy, that would be no joke. Those waves were huge out there.

It was so beautiful. But frightening, too. *Nothing to worry about, though,* she told herself. *We'll stay close to shore.*

"Was there something else you wanted to talk about?" Nathan said.

Daley cleared her throat. She was just on the edge of saying something. But she couldn't quite get there. What was she even going to say? *Never mind what I said the other day. Can I be your girlfriend after all?* God! Just the thought of it . . . it sounded so dumb and corny. Plus, she really wasn't sure that getting together with him on the island was a good idea anyway. In fact, she was pretty sure that—

"Daley?" Nathan said. "Was there something else?"

"Me? What? Oh, no, nothing else. Nothing at all. Why?"

Nathan cocked his head and looked at her for a minute. "I don't know," he said. "It just seemed like there was something you wanted to say."

Daley clapped him on the shoulder in what she hoped would seem like a sisterly way. "We better get back and eat so we can get to bed early. We're gonna need plenty of sleep tonight."

# THREE

**TWO WEEKS EARLIER**

*This isn't so bad,* Abby Fujimoto thought as she hiked through the forest. It was early in the day, and the oppressive tropical heat hadn't set in yet. Multicolored birds flitted through the air overhead, their raucous calls echoing happily through the trees.

Everywhere she looked, the world seemed new and exciting. Abby's family did a lot of camping and hiking, and she had been raised to believe that people should live in harmony with the natural world. What was there to worry about here? She'd been separated from Captain Russell and the others in a freak accident. It wouldn't happen again.

This time it would be . . . well, maybe "fun"

wasn't the right word. But it would be an interesting opportunity for personal growth. Right?

And not just that—she'd find the others and bring them back. Soon the whole group would be together. Maybe Captain Russell had figured out a way to get them off the island. Maybe all that was left to do was to reunite the two groups, and everything would be squared away again.

She hiked slowly up the next hill. The island was volcanic, so there were a lot of very steep hills. And this was the steepest one yet. *There's no rush,* she told herself. *It's all about the journey.* She pulled herself from tree to tree, vine to vine, rock to rock. When she needed a rest, she stopped briefly and took deep, cleansing breaths.

This was so much better, she thought, than sitting around cooped up in the camp with all the petty little jealousies and conflicts, waiting and waiting and waiting. Here, she felt like she was moving forward, making progress.

Finally she topped the rise, finding herself with a breathtaking view of the island. She surveyed the scene. From here she could see the mountain at the far end of the island. It was a little farther away than she'd thought. Higher, too. The flat, volcanic rim at the top was shrouded in clouds. A small waterfall cascaded over the side, the water turning to mist as it fell toward the emerald green jungle below.

*How many kids get to see something like this?* she thought. *I must be the luckiest girl in the world.* Eventually they'd all get off the island, and she'd look back at this moment as one of the best things that ever happened in her life.

On the far side of the mountain, she could see a crescent-shaped lagoon. A perfect place for Captain Russell and the others to camp and prepare their plans for getting off the island. She wasn't absolutely sure that's where they were. But she had a pretty good idea they'd be there.

The mountain was a little worrisome. She was going to have to swing wider to get around the steep volcanic sides of the peak. She had thought it would only take a day or so to get to the lagoon. But now that she looked at it from here, she revised her plans. Maybe more like two days. Three, tops. But that was okay. She'd packed plenty of water.

Speaking of which . . .

Realizing the hiking had made her a little thirsty, Abby reached into her pack to pull out her water. She'd packed a couple of bottles, plus a larger gallon-size container. She grabbed one of the bottles, screwed the top off, and took a long swig.

Perfect.

She put the bottle back. As she reached inside, though, her hand came away wet. She frowned. That was odd.

She felt the bottom of the pack. It was soaked. Where was the water coming from? With a slight pang of nervousness, she tugged on the gallon jug. It offered strangely little resistance. It should have been a lot heavier!

Abby yanked the plastic jug out of the backpack and found to her horror that it had a tiny little cut in the bottom, so small that it only dripped at a very slow rate. It must have been leaking since the minute she'd left. And now there was barely more than a couple of mouthfuls sloshing around in the bottom.

She stared. For a moment she had the urge to panic.

*Okay. Okay. Easy, Abby. No prob. Deep breaths. Think.*

After a few deep breaths she felt better. All those yoga classes she'd gone to with her mother were paying off. No point stressing out, right? She still had two quarts of water. There were streams on the island. It rained all the time here. The lagoon was only a couple of days away. What was she worried about? There was water everywhere.

Still . . . the thought crossed her mind that she could go back to camp and get more. It would be a lot easier to do that than to have to fool around with finding water.

But then she thought, *No, they wouldn't understand. They'd make a big scene.* She hated that kind of drama. She was all about harmony.

She carefully repacked the two quart bottles of water and began descending the hill. Nothing to worry about. Nature would provide.

Abby smiled. *I'll be fine,* she thought. *Of course I will!*

# FOUR

**THE PRESENT**

U nder Eric's watchful eye, the group dragged the raft down to the water. Eric was glad to see that the raft continued to seem very sturdy even when they moved it. None of the bamboo was cracking or shifting, none of the cross-braces were moving.

*Solid as a rock, baby!* Eric thought.

They reached the water and slid the little craft into the water. It floated beautifully, the deck bobbing well above the waterline. Eric just wished he could be on it.

"Here you go," Jackson said, handing a pair of paddles to Daley and Nathan. "I carved them myself last night."

"Wow!" Nathan said. "These look great."

"Thanks, Jackson," Daley said.

As Nathan and Daley strapped on the orange life preservers they'd taken from under the seats of the plane, Lex pointed at the sandbar. "Don't go too far out," he said. "Those waves are crashing pretty hard out there."

Everyone looked out to sea. The waves had gotten bigger since yesterday. Since they broke out on the sandbar, the waves were very gentle by the shore. But out there, they were pretty nasty looking. Eric felt a moment of concern for Daley and Nathan.

"Seriously, guys," Eric said. "I really didn't mean for you two to do this. Be careful."

"We know," Nathan said, looking him in the eye.

Eric felt almost like it was the first time Nathan had ever taken him seriously. He hated to admit it, but it was a good feeling.

"Pick a spot onshore and watch it," Lex said. "If there really is a current, you'll be able to gauge how far you've gone."

"No sweat, big guy," Nathan said, grinning. "Piece of cake."

"I'll be timing you," Lex said earnestly. "As soon as you pass the end of the beach, go ahead and bring the raft in. I measured the beach. It's about 1.6 kilometers long, and I can calculate with a good bit of precision just how fast the current is moving. That way we can measure—"

"We trust you with all the math, Lex," Eric said. "They need to get going, huh?"

Nathan and Daley put their paddles on top of the raft and began pushing it out into the water. Soon they were chest-deep in the water.

"Please be careful," Lex said.

"Good luck!" Melissa called.

Nathan and Daley clambered up onto the deck. It wobbled a little, and the raft sank much closer to the waterline. But all in all, it looked nice and stable.

Nathan threw Eric a thumbs-up, and then the pair began paddling. The raft moved out from the shore. It was working! And not only that, it was drifting rapidly down the shore. Everyone cheered.

"You timing this, Lex?" Eric said.

Lex nodded.

The small raft bobbed on the gentle waves, moving farther and farther away from the group of kids.

As Taylor watched Nathan and Daley moving swiftly offshore, a line formed between her eyebrows. "This is a good idea, isn't it?" she said.

"Absolutely," Eric said. "I mean . . . unless you want to spend the rest of your life on this island."

He looked around at the group. Everyone's faces looked tense and nervous.

"What?" Eric said. "They float to the end of the beach, they bail out, they swim for shore. What can go wrong?"

Nathan paddled with confidence. The oar that Jackson had made was working great. "This is awesome, huh?" he said. His legs were trailing in the water. It felt great—the cool water, the warm sun, the gentle breeze.

Daley flashed him a grin, then waved at the knot of kids back onshore. Everybody waved back. Lex began running down the shore, keeping pace with them.

"Look at that!" Daley said. "See how fast he's running? We're going even faster than him. We're really making progress."

"You think the current goes this fast all the way across the ocean?" Nathan said.

There was a brief silence.

"I mean, I hate to admit it," Nathan said. "But maybe Eric's right. Maybe this crazy thing could actually work."

"I don't know," Daley said. "If we missed Palau, we could be talking a couple hundred miles before we hit the Philippines. Even at this speed, that's a heck of a long way."

"True," Nathan said. He didn't really need to paddle anymore. They were moving comfortably along the shore. But it was kind of fun paddling. He liked the sensation of the paddle biting into the water, the feeling of the exercise. That was one of the things he missed about school. Regular exercise. There was a lot of work on the island . . . but not much time for regular exercise. Nathan took a deep breath and sighed with pleasure. "I'm kinda digging this."

"Yeah," Daley said. Then, after a pause, she added, "Alone at last."

Nathan turned and looked at her. Was she suggesting something? He thought that their whole conversation last week had resolved everything between them. "Huh?"

She poked him with the oar. "Hey, I'm *kidding.*"

After a minute, Lex stopped running. Melissa caught up with him. "Are they moving west?" she said.

Lex nodded. He was breathing hard from racing down the shoreline. "They're flying!" he said. "I can't believe how fast the current is moving them."

"Go west, my friends," Eric crowed. "Go west!"

"I can't watch this," Taylor said, putting her hands over her eyes.

"Look, I'm feeling a little woozy," Jackson said. "Even after two days of antibiotics, that giardia is still kicking my butt. I better go sit down for a minute."

"I'll go with you," Taylor said. "This is making me nervous."

For a few minutes, Daley and Nathan didn't speak. Daley enjoyed the gentle motion of the raft, the sun on her face. There was really nothing to do but relax.

She looked back at the beach. It was a lot farther away now. Melissa and Lex were trotting along the shoreline, following their progress. From out here, all their problems seemed a lot farther away.

"It really is beautiful here," Nathan said.

"It's paradise," Daley said. "Under the right circumstances, anyway."

Nathan laughed.

Daley looked behind the raft and saw a small piece of bamboo drifting slowly away from them. "Is that from us?" she said.

Nathan frowned. "Must be." He shook the raft a little. Everything seemed pretty solid. He shrugged. "Probably just a loose bundle somewhere in there. I wouldn't worry about it."

"I'm not worrying," Daley said. She let one leg trail in the water.

"Could we do this?" Nathan said. "I mean seriously? You think we could make a boat big enough and strong enough to make it across the Pacific Ocean?"

"I don't know. Maybe. There's a lot of bamboo on the island. There'd have to be room for provisions and water. We'd have to have some kind of shelter, too." She paused, thinking about it. Was it really that crazy of an idea? Crazier than sitting there waiting for help that didn't seem to be coming? "There's no way we could make a raft big enough for all of us, though."

"So who'd go?" said Nathan.

Daley felt a brief stab of fear in her gut. The idea of being out there in the middle of the ocean for that long? She had to admit, she wasn't that eager to try it. The ocean was great when your feet were touching the sand. But the farther out you got, the more powerful and uncontrollable and frightening the ocean became.

Back on the shore, Lex and Melissa looked like ants now. Daley looked to her left. They were getting awfully close to the sandbar. The heavy surf was breaking over the sand in huge curls of foaming white water.

"Uh . . ." she said. "You know, we're drifting kinda far out."

Nathan looked at the big waves and gulped. "Let's turn around."

Taylor helped Jackson to the shelter, where he slumped down against one of the posts. She was worried about him. He'd been chopping bamboo yesterday when he probably should have been lying in bed. Now he was paying the price.

"Thanks," he said wearily. "I feel good for a while, and then it just hits me."

Taylor poured him some water. "Here," she said. "This'll help."

"Thanks." Jackson sipped the water, then he closed his eyes for a minute.

Taylor put her hand on his forehead. There didn't seem to be any fever.

"That feels nice," he said.

Taylor held her hand there for as long as she could. Finally, though, she took it away. When they first got to the island, Jackson had kind of scared her. But now she was starting to get comfortable with him. Maybe a little *too* comfortable. Was she falling for the guy? No, that didn't make sense. He totally wasn't her type.

She stood up and looked out at the water. Through a gap in the trees, she could see the little raft bobbing along. It was surprisingly far away. Just the idea of being out there in all the deep water gave her the willies.

"Do you think they'll be okay?" Taylor asked.

"Yeah, they won't go far," Jackson said.

"So what if it works? Are we really going to build a raft and try to float home?"

"That is a very good question," Jackson said.

They were silent for a moment.

"Jackson?" Taylor said. "Be honest with me. Do you think they're still looking for us?"

Jackson opened his eyes and took another sip of the water. He didn't say anything for a moment. "Yeah," he said finally. "They're still looking."

Taylor suddenly felt her eyes growing watery. "Don't just say that because it's what I want to hear!"

"Look, eleven people disappeared. Ten of 'em are kids. Nathan's dad is the district attorney of Los Angeles County. Daley's dad is some famous filmmaker. Your dad's the richest guy in California."

"Second richest," Taylor corrected him.

Jackson's eyes popped open. "Only the *second* richest?" He sighed dramatically. "Oh, forget it then. Nobody will care. I guess we're done for."

"Shut up!" Taylor laughed and slapped him playfully on the arm. The more she got to know Jackson, the better she liked him. He came off kind of sullen at first. But after you got to know him, you realized he was kind of a funny guy.

"Seriously, though," Jackson said. "I bet your dad's got ten planes in the air flying all over the Pacific right now. They just haven't gotten here yet."

Lex, Eric, and Melissa were still following Daley and Nathan as the current drove them down the shoreline. Lex was getting worried.

"They're too far out," he said.

Melissa didn't say anything . . . but it was obvious from the worried expression on her face that she agreed.

"Hey!" Lex shouted. "Come back in! You're too close to the waves."

Lex and Melissa both started waving their arms and shouting. But there was no indication that Daley and Nathan could hear them. They were still just floating along like nothing was happening.

Eric didn't say anything. But he was looking a little nervous, too.

"This is torture," Melissa said. "What if something happens to them?"

The raft was now approaching the end of the beach where a spit of rough volcanic rock projected far out into the water. Once it passed the tip of the land there, Nathan and Daley would disappear from view.

"Did anybody bring their shoes?" Lex said. His own feet were bare, as were those of the older kids.

"Why?" Eric said.

"We need to cross that rock so we can see them." Lex pointed at the razor-sharp rocks in front of them.

"Well, it's not like we can swim out to them if something happens," Eric said. "Anyway, look at them. They're doing fine."

They all turned to look.

But Daley and Nathan were gone.

"I'm gonna go get the first-aid kit," Melissa said.

"What for?" Eric said.

"I don't know!"

Lex's heart was pounding now. He wasn't sure if it was because of all the running. Or because he was scared about what might happen to his sister.

Nathan started paddling hard toward the land. As did Daley. But it didn't seem to make any difference at all. They were still racing along the shore, moving ever closer to the huge waves. Nathan could hear the ominous thudding of the surf now, and a haze of mist was drifting toward them, thrown up by the waves breaking on the sandbar.

"The current is really strong," Nathan said. For the first time since they'd gone out, he was starting to feel genuinely scared. He had done a little surfing in the summers. The biggest waves he'd surfed were about half the size of the ones that were rolling in off the ocean now. And those waves had terrified him.

"I can't believe we didn't think of this!" Daley said. "Now we have to paddle against it."

The two dug into the water, paddling for all they

were worth. Slowly, slowly they began to make progress toward the shore. But Nathan could feel his arms burning, his back stiffening up, pain radiating into his neck. He wasn't sure how long he could keep up this pace.

"Paddle harder!" Daley yelled, her face full of grim determination.

"We've got to pace ourselves," Nathan called back to her. He kept paddling, but he eased up the tempo, not digging quite so deep into the water.

Out of the corner of his eye, though, he could see that Daley was fighting with every ounce of her strength, plunging the paddle into the ocean all the way to the handle. He was worried she'd exhaust herself if she wasn't careful.

"Ease up," he said. "Just a little."

But that wasn't Daley's way of doing things. All or nothing—that was Daley for you. You had to admire her. He smiled faintly. She was paddling so hard that the raft was starting to curve in his direction. Nathan was now looking toward the beach. Well . . . he was looking where the beach *had* been. But they'd passed the point where the lava had once flowed into the ocean, and now they were moving out to sea.

He could actually see the track of the current. The swiftly moving water had picked up silt along the beach, leaving a dark river in the ocean.

This was more than just an ocean current. It

was practically a riptide. As it passed around the volcanic point, he could see that the riptide left a sheltered area by the shore where the water didn't appear to be moving at all. If they could just get out of the dark current, they'd be okay. Maybe a hundred yards? Two hundred? Problem was, every second was taking them farther out to sea.

He paddled a few more strokes, straightening them out, then turned to look out at the surf, hoping they'd made some progress. They had. The big waves had retreated a little. For a minute or two, he'd been afraid that an especially big wave might come along and turn them over. But now they were definitely out of danger from the waves.

But as he looked to his left, he realized there was another problem, something that made his heart sink.

"Uh-oh," he said.

Jackson was puzzled by Taylor. Mostly she seemed totally oblivious and dopey. But was that just a pose? Sometimes she seemed like she was hiding her real character behind the veneer of the annoying rich girl. Hard to tell. But she rarely showed any vulnerability at all. He was a little surprised to see her putting a finger to each eye, trying to stifle the tears.

"We're gonna make it home, Taylor," he said. "One way or another."

Taylor wiped her eyes, then sat up a little straighter. "Tell you what. I'm going to do my best to believe that."

Jackson smiled. "There you go."

Taylor sighed loudly and leaned toward him, resting her chin in her hands. "When this is over, are we still going to be friends?"

Jackson cleared his throat, not quite sure where she was going with this. "You mean . . . like, all of us? Or you and me?"

Taylor moved closer to him, rested her head on his shoulder. He could feel her long hair spilling down his arm. He wasn't quite sure how to react. So he just patted her gently on the arm.

She didn't stir, just closed her eyes.

Jackson felt strange about this whole thing. Was Taylor just looking for a shoulder to lean on . . . literally? Or was she kinda digging him?

He didn't really have the energy to think about it. That giardia had just knocked the wind out of him. He felt a wave of fatigue wash over him. He let his eyes close.

Melissa rushed over the small dunes between the beach and the shelter. The first-aid kit was usually in the tent. But sometimes people took it out to—

Suddenly she screeched to a stop.

There in front of her were Jackson and Taylor. Taylor rested her head on Jackson's shoulder, her long blond hair spilling down over the right side of his chest, one hand resting idly on his leg.

What in the—

Taylor? And Jackson? She felt sick.

Jackson—who was so deep and thoughtful? With Taylor? Who was so . . . *not*? How *could* he?

It was just wrong!

And Jackson had made such a big deal with her about how they couldn't get together because it would be too complicated and all this stuff. It had all been bogus, hadn't it? He'd just been chicken and didn't want to tell her that he didn't like her that way.

The first-aid kit lay on the floor of the shelter at Jackson's feet. She grabbed the kit, then ran toward the beach, her mind going numb. She couldn't think about Jackson right now. Not with Daley and Nathan out there in the water.

Lex and Eric were waiting for her at the edge of the old lava flow that extended out into the water.

"Well," she said. "I got the first-aid kit."

Eric looked nervously at the black jagged surface of the volcanic rock next to them. "So . . . what do we do now?"

"We find a way across it," she said firmly. She was surprised at how calm she felt, how clearly she seemed to be thinking.

"Right!" Lex said.

She put one foot on the rock. Tiny sharp projections bit into her feet. She took another step.

"Well?" she said. "Let's go."

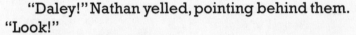

"Daley!" Nathan yelled, pointing behind them. "Look!"

"Keep . . . paddling . . . Nathan!" she yelled. Her voice was hoarse and her breath was coming so hard that she could barely say more than one word at a time.

"Daley! Stop!"

He kept pointing.

Finally Daley stopped paddling. She looked behind them. For a moment her face was blank.

"Oh my God," she said.

A trail of bamboo and vines spread out behind them, bobbing gently in the waves.

"We're coming apart," Nathan said.

# FIVE

**TWO WEEKS EARLIER**

**B**y the second day, Abby had reached the edge of the mountain. Occasionally when the clouds parted, she could see a thin trail of smoke coming from the peak. The volcano up there must still be active.

On the first day she might have taken some time to appreciate the magnificence of the view. But after hiking up and down and up and down and up and down through jungle for a whole day, and then getting zero sleep as she lay on the dirt, hearing freaky noises in the trees, and feeling bugs crawl across her skin—well, the beauties of nature were seeming a lot less interesting.

Plus, she was running low on water. She hadn't quite realized just how much energy it took to climb these hills. And in this heat, energy meant sweat. And sweat meant dehydration.

She had yet to find a stream anywhere. There was no sign of rain, not a cloud in the sky.

Abby sat down on an outcropping of rock and looked up at the sheer walls of rock towering over her. It was a giant canyon. A dead end.

Her plan had been to skirt around the bottom of the mountain. But now that she was here, she had a feeling that she'd made a terrible mistake. The mountain was just one cliff after another, with steep runners of volcanic rock plummeting down at angles too sharp to navigate on foot.

She should have swung wide over gentler terrain. It would have been longer as the crow flies. But it would have taken a lot less time.

Now she was going to have to retrace her steps. She'd wasted the last two hours. Maybe more.

She held up her last bottle of water. It was a quarter full.

There was no question in her mind that she was still a solid day away from the lagoon. A quarter of a bottle of water? Maybe you could get by on that back home, sitting around in an air-conditioned house. But here? No way.

Unless there was a rainstorm or unless she found a stream—she was in trouble.

Big trouble.

For a moment she had an urge to go plunging

through the woods, screaming for help. *Yeah. Like that would help.*

She turned around, hefted her pack, and began walking back the way she'd come. Trying to keep her strides slow and calm. *Deep breaths,* she told herself. *Deep breaths.*

# SIX

## THE PRESENT

**W**ith a groan and a creak, the raft settled into the water like a balloon deflating.

And then, in the space of no more than ten seconds, it was no longer a raft at all, just a scattering of junk floating in the middle of a vast, open stretch of water.

"It's okay . . . it's . . . okay!" Daley gasped. She didn't look okay, though. "We've got . . . life vests on. We can . . . just . . . swim for it." There was an edge of panic to her voice, and she didn't seem to be able to catch her breath.

Nathan shook his head. "No," he said. "We're not gonna make it."

"What do you mean?" Daley asked, her head

just bobbing above the water.

"Look," Nathan said. "The current's pushing us out to sea. Pretty soon we'll pass the end of the island. And then we're cooked."

"But—"

"Can you see back there? The current is getting pushed out by the point at the end of the beach. It's basically a riptide. We have to make it through that riptide. Can you see it?"

"I can't ... see ... anything!" Nathan knew Daley was an excellent swimmer. But she had obviously exhausted herself by paddling too hard. A small wave broke over her head.

For a brief second Nathan felt something under his feet. The sandbar! For a moment it made him feel good. If they could get their feet under them, then maybe—

He looked to his left. No, forget it. Never mind. The sandbar wasn't going to help them. They were getting sucked out toward the big waves. By the time they were able to walk on the sandbar, they'd be getting crushed by every wave that came by. *Oh, man!* he thought. The waves were the biggest he'd ever seen in his life.

He had to think of something. Now!

He reached out for Daley. Another wave roared over her head. She came up tossing her hair and spluttering, eyes wide.

"Nathan!" she called. "What are we gonna do?"

Toward the shore he could see . . . the end of the island! They weren't there yet. But if they didn't hurry—

And then, suddenly, it came to him, the thing they had to do.

"Take off your life vest!" he shouted.

"What?" Daley stared at him. "No, we're—"

Another wave passed over their heads. They still weren't directly under the crashing waves. But they were getting close.

"Do it!" he shouted. "Now!"

Melissa picked her way slowly through the rocks. She'd seen this guy walking on glass on TV one time. He'd said the trick was to slowly put your foot down, spreading the weight across your whole foot.

"Ow!" Eric said. "Ow, ow, ow!"

"Yeesh," Lex said. "I think I just cut my foot."

"I can't do this," Eric said.

"Hey, you got them into this," Melissa said. "The least you can do is cross fifty feet of sharp rock."

"Sharp rock? Fifty feet of broken glass is more like it!" But Eric kept going.

Melissa finally reached the top of the lava flow and looked out at the beach to the left. For a moment she couldn't see anything. And then, when she finally did see it, she was almost sorry she did.

"Oh no," she said.

Lex came over the hill. Then Eric.

Then they saw it, too. There was no raft anymore. Just a jumble of bamboo off in the distant water, being pounded and crushed and torn apart by the surf.

"No!" Eric screamed. "No! It can't be!"

"Keep going," Melissa said coldly.

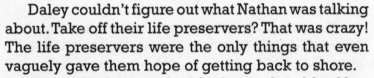

Daley couldn't figure out what Nathan was talking about. Take off their life preservers? That was crazy! The life preservers were the only things that even vaguely gave them hope of getting back to shore.

"Now!" Nathan reached for her and grabbed her arm. "Take it off!"

"No!" she screamed back.

Strangely, Nathan seemed to be standing up in the water now. His fingers closed around her arm, holding her firmly. The current was rushing around them. Huh? Why weren't they moving with the current? It took her a moment to get it: They must have just hit the sandbar.

She put her feet down, felt the sand with her toes. *Thank God! Solid ground!*

But then the next wave hit them and she lost her footing.

When she surfaced, Nathan was still gripping her arm, his fingers digging into her skin. She had never been so glad to feel pain in her life. He was holding her fast again, resisting the swiftly moving current, his body braced against the water.

"Daley!" he shouted. "Do you trust me?" His large brown eyes stared desperately into hers.

"What?"

"Do you trust me?"

"Yeah, but—"

"Then do what I say," he shouted.

Another wave knocked them over, spun them around. But Nathan never let go.

As their heads came up out of the water, Nathan said, "There's no time. We can't stay here. Each time the waves hit us, they push us farther. We'll just wear ourselves out."

"But—"

"Take it off!" With his free hand, Nathan was already jerking his own life preserver off.

"I don't understand!"

A giant wall of water raised up in front of them, then crashed on the sandbar not more than thirty feet from them. The foam raced toward them.

"If you trust me, then do it."

For a moment Daley felt almost giddy. *What am I thinking? Trust him with my life? I don't trust anybody that much!*

But then she looked into his eyes again, and

suddenly she felt something that she hadn't felt in years—not since her mom died. A sense of release. Letting herself go. Letting someone else carry the load.

She began fumbling with the buckles on her life vest. As the roiling water surged around her, stripping the life preserver from her shoulders and sucking it away, she thought, *Oh God. What have I just done?*

Melissa could see two dots of orange among the jumble of bamboo floating rapidly down the beach. *Those must be their life preservers,* she thought.

As long as they had the life preservers, they should be okay. Right?

The orange dots were being sucked toward the surf now, the huge waves that were breaking way offshore on the sandbar. Those waves would be paradise for surfers. But if you were just trying to swim out there, they'd probably beat you to pieces.

Plus the current was moving so swiftly, it was liable to propel them past the end of the island. They were still a pretty long way from the end of the island, but the current seemed to be driving them out to sea.

She squinted, trying to see the life preservers

more clearly. To her horror, she realized that there was no one in the life preservers. They were empty, floating on the water. Where were Nathan and Daley? It seemed like they were just ... *gone*!

Heedless of the sharp rocks jabbing into her feet, she began to run.

# SＥＶＥＮ

**TWO WEEKS EARLIER**

As the day wore on, Abby realized that she was getting lost. As long as she could see the mountain, she was okay. But most of the time, the peak was hidden from her by the jungle and by the steep hills she was climbing. And with the sun almost directly overhead, it was impossible to tell east from west.

Several times she felt almost certain she had gotten turned around, circling through the same series of hills and valleys, ending up in the same spot.

But she wasn't completely sure. She was so tired and confused that it could have been her imagination. Why hadn't she thought to bring a compass? There were two or three of them back in the camp. She could have just grabbed one and no one would have even noticed.

Abby didn't consider herself to be a resentful person. But as she climbed up one hill and down the next, her arms and legs getting cut on branches, her muscles aching, her feet blistering—she began to have a bad taste in her mouth every time she thought of them. They were back at Camp Fat 'n Happy with their feet up, doing nothing to get rescued, just waiting around for help that might never come. Plenty of food, plenty of water, a couple of waterproof tents, sleeping bags, a nice fire—living like kings! It didn't seem fair.

Eventually Abby stopped and opened her pack. She'd eaten more food than she had expected to yesterday. She was down to dried fruit and a pack of crackers. And maybe one tablespoon of water.

She shoved two crackers into her mouth and started chewing. But when she tried to swallow—the crackers wouldn't move. Her mouth was so dry that trying to swallow the crackers made her gag. She put a tiny bit of water in her mouth, just enough to turn the crackers into paste. She choked the crackers down, then ate a slice of dried mango. There was the tiniest, tiniest bit of moisture in it. But even so, it was hard to get it down. She looked at her water bottle. A few drops and that was it.

She dropped two drops onto her tongue. It was enough for her to get the mango down. She checked the other bottle. *Wow,* she thought greedily. *There's almost a teaspoon of water!*

She was still absolutely ravenous, though. She jammed several more crackers in her mouth, chewed them thoroughly, and tried to swallow.

But it was like having sand in her mouth. The crackers just sat there on her tongue. For two minutes she tried and tried to swallow. But it was no good.

It struck her that if she didn't find water soon— before the end of the day—she was not going to make it. Suddenly her eyes felt hot and she began to cry. Reaching up to wipe the tears away, she found that her eyes were completely dry. She was so dehydrated that her body couldn't even spare the water to make tears.

She made a choking noise and the crackers began spilling out of her mouth like fine white dust, drifting slowly toward the ground.

*Water. I've got to find water.*

She pushed herself to her feet, shouldered her bag, and looked around. Which way had she been going? That way? No, wait. That way?

She began stumbling up the ridge.

*I don't even know where I'm going,* she thought.

Abby made it up one ridge. At the top of the ridge, she caught a glimpse of the mountain. The high waterfall cascaded down and down toward the base of the mountain, all the water disappearing in a cloud of vapor. A rainbow moved and shimmered inside the falling water.

Yesterday it had seemed so beautiful. Now it just seemed like some kind of torture, knowing that all that water up there was going to waste. It was way too far away for her to hike to.

But still, her mind drifted, and she imagined herself under the cascade, arms outstretched, mouth open, feeling the cool water spilling down over her, filling her . . .

*Why can't I be there?* she thought. *Why can't I have that?*

She began to walk down the ridge. Then she stumbled and started to fall. She tried to stop herself, but she had no energy left.

It didn't even really hurt. The spongy soil was relatively soft, and the hillside wasn't that steep. She just rolled and rolled. It seemed almost like slow motion, the green world spinning around her. Spinning and spinning.

And then when she hit bottom, she just stopped and lay there. Above her was a large banana plant. She could see the bananas up in the tree. Vaguely, in some deep recess of her mind, it occurred to her that bananas had moisture in them. They were food and water in one neat little yellow package.

*Get up,* she thought. *Get up! Get the banana.*

But the banana tree seemed very far away. She lay there staring at the patches of sky that peeped around the long, broad leaves of the tree. It was a cheerful blue. After a while, it changed color, growing darker. Finally the sky turned black.

Huh, she thought vaguely. *Isn't that funny. The sky is black.*

# EIGHT

**THE PRESENT**

Daley watched the life preserver disappear into the crashing surf. It seemed like all her hope went with it.

"What are we *doing*, Nathan?" she screamed.

Nathan was still holding tight to her arm. "Look, the current runs really fast between the sandbar and the shore. Out beyond the surf, I bet the current's a lot slower."

"But—"

Another wave washed over them.

Nathan came up spluttering. "We're going to have to swim *under* the waves. With the life preservers on, we'd never make it. We'd be stuck on top of the water, where the waves are crashing."

Daley nodded. She still didn't see the sense of

it. Even if Nathan was right, the current out there would eventually pull them out to sea. "But ... that just takes us deeper into the ocean."

"I know."

"We'll be stuck out there! We'll just drown out there!"

Nathan shook his head. "Trust me," he said. "I know what I'm doing." He looked behind them. Another huge wave was crashing onto the sandbar about twenty or thirty feet away. "Duck!" he said.

Then he disappeared under the water. Daley blinked. What was he doing? It didn't make sense.

But she followed him anyway, ducking deep down into the water. She could hear the remains of the big wave rushing over them. It tugged hard at her. But it wasn't as strong down toward the bottom as it was on the top. She sank her hands and feet into the sand. The wave didn't move her an inch.

*Okay,* she thought. *Maybe there's some method to his madness.*

After the wave passed, she rose up out of the water, gasping for breath. She was still worn out from paddling. She wasn't sure how many times she'd be able to do this. The current was still moving really fast. This was like holding onto the edge of a cliff. You could only do it for so long. But eventually they'd just have to let go.

When Nathan surfaced he said, "Wait until the next wave goes by. The second it passes, get underwater and swim like mad."

"But—"

"We have to pass through the break point."

"Break point?"

"That's a surfer word. It means the place where the wave starts to turn over and crash down on you. If it breaks on us, we're cooked. Even underwater."

"I still don't understand what good this is gonna do us!"

"I have a plan!" Nathan yelled. Over Nathan's shoulder, Daley could see a huge wave rearing up. It looked impossibly high. How could they swim under something like that? It seemed as big as a house.

The wave curled over, then thundered down over the sandbar. Daley could feel the impact in her chest.

"Duck!" Nathan yelled again.

Again Daley went down. Again she plunged her hands and feet into the sand. Again, what was left of the wave passed over them.

When she surfaced, Nathan was already waiting. "Okay, one more wave," he said. "See that one?" Nathan pointed out to sea. "That's a small one. I think we can make it under that."

Daley gulped. The wave he was pointing at sure didn't look small to her. A small *house*, maybe.

"The exact second that the first wave passes over you, start swimming out under the water. If we do it right, we'll hit the break point just before it rolls over."

"Okay." Daley felt like something was squeezing her chest. Her pulse was hammering in her ears. And she felt so tired. She wasn't sure she'd have the strength—or the breath—to make it to the break point.

"Look at me," Nathan said. His brown eyes bored into her. "You can do it. You're the toughest girl I've ever met in my life. You can *do* it!"

And for a second, she believed it.

Then the next wave hit.

"Get ready!" Nathan said.

"But what are we gonna do when we get out there?"

Nathan yelled, "We're gonna—"

But whatever it was he was about to say, he didn't have a chance. The next wave hit them and Nathan's head disappeared under the water. Daley dropped down, dug into the sand, and felt the roaring water pass over her.

*Now!* she thought. *Swim!*

"Where are they? Where are they?" Lex yelled.

Melissa wasn't sure. All she knew was that she

had to run as fast as she could. She was off of the volcanic rock now, pounding down the hard wet sand, heading toward where the life rafts and the bamboo were.

She ran and ran, her head swimming with terrible thoughts.

Nathan was her best friend. They'd known each other since they were in kindergarten. The notion that in the space of a few seconds he could just disappear into the sea? It didn't even make sense.

"Melissa!" Eric's voice pursued her down the beach. "Melissa, your feet are bleeding!"

*My feet are bleeding?* Sometimes she wondered about Eric. How could anybody possibly think that her feet were important at a moment like this?

She kept running and running. Her eyes never left the water, not for a second. Her eyes were fastened on the life preservers. Even if they'd lost the vests, they had to be close by. As fast as she ran, the two orange dots seemed to be moving even faster.

If she could just get there, she resolved that she'd swim out and try to save them. Even if she didn't make it.

"Melissa!" This time it was Lex calling. "Melissa! Stop!"

*I know my feet are bleeding! I don't care!* She just kept putting one foot in front of the other, her breath coming in a chest full of knives.

"Melissa! Stop! I see them!"

Melissa came to a halt and whirled around. Behind her Lex was standing on the sand, pointing straight out from the beach.

She looked out into the ocean. She couldn't believe it. He was right! Two heads appeared and disappeared. They didn't seem to be moving with the current, either. They were almost out to the huge waves, though.

"They're on the sandbar," Lex called.

She stared. They were so far out, they looked like ants. But they were *there*. It was definitely Nathan and Daley. She felt a rush of relief.

"Thank God!" she said. "They're gonna be okay."

Lex didn't say anything for a minute. Finally he spoke. "No," he said. "They're trapped."

"What do you mean?"

"The current?" he said. "It's a riptide. See that dark streak running parallel to the beach? That's the riptide. When the current comes around the volcanic point that we just walked over, it gets compressed. It accelerates. It's very interesting, actually—the Bernoulli Principle states that—" He clapped himself on the forehead. "What am I talking about? Who cares about the Bernoulli Principle."

"But why are they trapped?"

"Well, the current is going so fast, I think that it'll take them out to sea if they try to swim across it." He pointed farther down the beach. The island curved inward, the beach disappearing to the north. "See down there, the sandbar disappears and the riptide just keeps going straight out into the ocean. It'll slow down once it passes the end of the island. But by then they may be too far out to swim all the way back."

"What are we gonna do?" Melissa wailed.

Lex didn't answer. He seemed transfixed by something out there in the ocean.

"What is it?" Melissa asked, turning back toward Daley and Nathan. But then she knew why he was staring. Daley and Nathan had disappeared.

"Where'd they go?" Melissa felt frantic. "They got sucked under!"

Eric finally jogged up next to them, panting. "I don't think so," he said, his chest heaving. "I think they're swimming out."

"Out?" Melissa said. "But . . . they'd be swimming out into those huge waves."

"That doesn't make any sense," Eric said.

For a moment they all just stared at the empty ocean. Melissa felt like she couldn't breathe.

Suddenly a head popped up at the top of one of the giant waves, just on the other side of the sandbar. Then a second head appeared.

Eric cheered.

Melissa looked at him soberly. "I don't know why you're so happy," she said. "They'll never get in now." It wasn't Melissa's way to get mad at people. But she couldn't help blaming him for what had happened.

Eric's face fell. He put his hands over his eyes. "You're right. You're right. This is all my fault."

"Why did they do that?" Melissa said. "Why did they swim out? It's crazy."

Suddenly Lex's eyes widened, like he'd just realized something. "Maybe not," he said softly.

"What do you mean?" Eric said. "What are they doing out there?"

Lex smiled slightly. "I think they're gonna go surfing!"

Nathan felt a burst of triumph. Daley was treading water right next to him. They'd made it!

Then Nathan looked behind them and saw the next wave rearing up over them. They were past the break point—barely. But the waves were freakin' enormous. A frigid wave of fear ran through him. People just weren't supposed to be around waves this big. A wave this big could toss a school bus and crush it like an eggshell.

He glanced at Daley. Her face was pale. He'd never seen her look like this. She looked terrified. He reached out and touched her arm. Her skin felt cold and rubbery in the water.

"What are we doing?" she said.

Suddenly the big wave was on them and they

rose up like they were on an elevator. "Whoa!" Nathan said. "Man, that was kind of a big one."

"Nathan, they're all big." She tossed her red hair back. "Now, what are we doing? The current's got us again."

Nathan's heart was pounding. "You ever been bodysurfing?"

"Sometimes when I go to the beach, yeah."

"Well, that's what we're gonna do. We're gonna catch a wave, and we're gonna ride it. We're gonna ride it across the sandbar, and we're gonna keep riding it." He pointed as they rose on another massive wave. "Watch what they do."

The wave crashed in front of them, roiled over the sandbar, and then kept going, a much smaller wave now, but still moving, crossing the dark surface of the riptide.

"If we can stay with the wave," Nathan said, "cross the sandbar, then keep going. See? See, that wave will cross the rip in about . . ." He counted as the small wave pushed through the riptide. "One, two, three, four, five, six, seven."

"Seven seconds!" Daley grinned as the wave pushed out of the darker water of the rip and into the stiller ocean closer to shore. "Nathan, you're a genius!" Then her grin faded. "But . . . can we make it over the sandbar? If it crashes on top of us . . ."

She didn't finish the sentence. Another wave propelled them up and up, then dropped them again.

"Don't think about that," Nathan said. "We're gonna have to chance it and hope we can stay ahead of the curl. If we can stay on the front of the wave, we'll be able to get through it. No problem." He wasn't as sure as he made it sound. But he wasn't going to admit that to Daley.

"I'm not even sure I can do this," Daley said. "I haven't bodysurfed in a long time. You have to time it exactly right or you won't catch the wave."

Nathan nodded. "That's why you're gonna listen to me. As the wave comes in, we'll just put our heads down and go. You gotta paddle like crazy. Then as soon as you feel the wave catching you, put your head down and your hands out, and point your toes. Once the wave's got you, don't look up. Don't look up whatever you do. You'll stall out and the wave will smash you to bits."

"Head down, arms out, point the toes."

"Once we clear the sandbar, keep your head down and keep kicking so you stay with the wave. Count to seven. Keep kicking and kicking until you get to seven. Then we should be clear of the rip."

"Count to seven and keep kicking," she repeated. She sounded almost like she was in a trance.

Nathan nodded. He squeezed her arm. "We're gonna make it!"

Daley winced. He really was putting a death grip on her arm. "Sorry," he said.

"I'm fine," she said.

"Exactly when I go," Nathan said. "Not one second earlier, not one second later. *Exactly.*"

Daley nodded.

"We're gonna be like one person, okay, Daley? Then we'll be fine."

In front of them, a wave rose up and up. As it thinned out, Daley could see sunlight through the water. It was like a giant blue wall. For a moment she felt paralyzed. *This is ridiculous,* she thought. *This is so totally impossible.*

But then Nathan reached out and squeezed her arm again.

"With me," he said softly. His voice was calm and assured. "One. Two. With me. With me . . ."

She felt the wave lifting them. There was a white feathering of foam at the crest, impossibly high above them.

*"Now!"*

He barely had time to get in more than three strokes before the wave pitched them over and rocketed them forward. He could feel Daley next to him, matching him stroke for stroke. They could have been part of some machine, their actions were so alike.

Then as the wave took over, he sucked in air, put his head down, and Daley disappeared. He jammed his hands out in front of him, arched his back slightly, and shoved his legs out straight, pointing his toes.

And then he was just part of the wave.

Nathan had surfed enough to know that strange mix of terror and jubilation that always came over you when you rode a good wave.

But nothing like this.

This was a whole new thing. The wave was so fast that it felt like being in a sports car when someone stomps on the accelerator and the car pins you back in your seat. And as soon as he felt the power of the wave, he felt sure they'd never make it. It was just too big, too strong. They'd slide back up inside the curl, get thrown over the top, and be smashed like toys on the sandbar.

But still he kept his position, kicking with his legs as hard as he could, trying to keep low and forward on the wave. It was the most amazing thing he'd ever done.

*Well,* he thought, *if I gotta check out now, I couldn't have picked a better way to go.*

Then he heard thunder, felt the wave smashing around him, the concussion of the water slamming deep inside his chest. The front of the wave was pulling at him, sucking him up into the break. He kicked and kicked and kicked, fighting off the tug of the water.

And just as he thought he'd lost the war against the wave, it was over.

The wave relaxed, the thunder abated, and they were past the sandbar.

But now his air was giving out. The effort of keeping himself in front of the wave had sucked most of the oxygen out of his lungs. But he knew that he couldn't put his head up. Not till he'd made it all the way through the riptide. He counted as he kicked.

One. Two. Three.

His chest was burning. He felt like the water was pressing in on him now. But still the wave propelled him on.

Four. Five.

*Air! Air! I need air!*

Six. Seven.

He couldn't hold it anymore. He put up his head and sucked in air.

"Omigod!" Melissa shouted. "Omigod! Omigod!"

Daley and Nathan were swimming through the ocean next to each other, not five feet apart, two silver streaks cutting across the dark water.

Lex put his arms around Melissa. "Come on, Daley! Come on, Nathan!" he screamed.

Eric had his hands over his face, peeking out

through his fingers with one eye.

Melissa could see their arms extended, their feet pumping as they rode the wave through the dark water that outlined the riptide. She could sense the difficulty of it, the need for air, the need to ride it all the way into the still blue water closer to shore. They were still a long way out.

"Come on, guys. Come on!" Eric said.

And suddenly their heads both popped up. Right where the dark water turned to a safer, calmer blue.

"They made it!" Melissa screamed. She started jumping up and down. A burst of pure joy ran through her. "They made it!"

Eric and Lex and Melissa hugged one another, all of them jumping up and down in unison.

Finally they stopped and looked out at the water again. "Hmm," Lex said. "They still have kind of a long way to go. I hope they didn't wear themselves out."

Nathan finally looked up and saw that Daley had made it, too. She was a little behind him. But not far. He could see they had just reached the edge of the riptide. The water was still moving around them . . . but not too quickly.

"We did it!" he called with a grin.

Daley smiled wanly. She didn't look so good.

Her face was pale and drawn, and she was spluttering and gasping, her head barely clear of the water.

"Are you okay?"

Daley winced. "I've got a cramp. I don't think . . . I can make it." For a moment she slipped under the water.

Nathan swam rapidly to her.

She surfaced again briefly. "The current's too strong!" she said. "It's too deep. I can't swim against it."

"Don't even try," he said. He didn't feel real calm . . . but he knew that if they were going to make it to shore, he'd have to keep *her* calm. "Don't struggle. Just turn over on your back and kick your legs a little. I'll do the rest."

It was the sort of thing that Daley normally would have immediately declined. But right now she was obviously in no mood to argue. He slipped in behind her, put his arm across her chest, and started towing her.

"We're not far from shore," he said.

"Don't tell me," she said. "Lifeguard merit badge, right?"

"Lifesaving, actually." It was hard to talk. He was getting pretty worn out.

"Gotta love the Boy Scouts."

He swam a few more strokes. He hadn't realized just how much those huge waves had taken out of him. "Daley . . . I . . . I don't know if I can go much farther."

"It's okay," she said. "I just needed a little rest. I think I can make it the rest of the way."

Gratefully Nathan let go of her, turned around, and began a slow breaststroke toward shore.

"They're still drifting," Eric said, watching as Nathan towed Daley through the choppy surf.

"I think they'll make it, though," Melissa said. Nathan and Daley were almost there.

"We're gonna be blocked off from them again," Lex said, pointing.

At the far end, the beach curved around and disappeared behind a dune. Melissa realized he was right. Just past the dune, there was another outcropping of rock they'd have to get over.

The three made their way to the rock as Nathan and Daley disappeared behind the dune.

"Hurry," Melissa said urgently. Now that it looked like Nathan and Daley would be all right, she was starting to feel the pain in her feet. Fortunately the rock on this outcropping looked a lot less hard on the feet than the other one. It was just a jumble of large boulders that had been worn smooth by the sea.

She began making her way over the rocks.

"Oh, man!" Nathan said. "Now *I've* got a cramp." Suddenly it felt like a pair of scissors was embedded in his right lung. He felt for the bottom with his toes. There was sand down there. But it was too deep to keep his head clear of the water.

"Turn around," Daley said.

Nathan turned and felt Daley's arm across his chest. Now she was towing him. He kicked his feet just enough to keep them from sinking. It took only a few strokes. Then Daley said, "I think we're okay."

Nathan almost wished they had a little farther to go. He kind of liked the feel of her arm across his chest. But then she let go. He let his feet sink . . . and there it was. Hard, firm sand.

The pair staggered through the waves, propping each other up, and then finally fell onto the sand together.

After a few seconds, Nathan looked over at Daley. She was breathing hard and still looking a little pale. Suddenly they both burst into laughter. They'd made it! They'd really made it! Daley was looking straight into his eyes.

Then she leaned forward and they hugged, clenching onto each other tightly. Nathan felt relief flooding through him. But not just relief. There was something else, a feeling of closeness that was like nothing he'd felt with Daley before. For just a moment, all the awkwardness and uncertainty between them vanished.

"Nathan," Daley said, "I mean this from the bottom of my heart. I don't know what I'd do without you."

Nathan felt his eyes widen. He'd never heard Daley say anything like that before. He felt like he could just sit here forever, holding onto her.

Suddenly there was a commotion coming from farther down the beach. "Look," a voice called. "There they are!"

Nathan and Daley quickly let go of each other. It was Melissa calling. Behind her Lex and Eric appeared over the top of a jumble of large boulders.

They ran quickly across the short stretch of sand.

"Oh, man," Eric said. "You don't know how glad I am to see you guys."

"Daley!" Lex yelled, throwing his arms around his sister's shoulders.

Nathan felt a little weird that the others might have seen them hugging, so he stood up quickly and started brushing the sand off his pants.

"We're fine!" Daley said brusquely. It was obvious from the expression on her face that she was feeling a little odd, too. She cleared her throat. "So, uh, the good news is that there's definitely a current. And it's heading straight west."

"The bad news," Nathan added, "is that the raft needs a little work."

"I would have drowned if it hadn't been for Nathan," Daley said.

"I don't know about that," Nathan said. "But, yeah, the raft is a problem."

"So should I be happy or upset?" Eric said.

"Neither," Melissa said. It was the first time she had spoken since she arrived. "It just means that nothing has changed."

Nathan looked at her curiously. She seemed unusually distant. Especially given that they'd almost died out there.

"I'm glad everybody's fine," she said in a monotone voice. Then she turned and started trudging up the beach.

Melissa had seen it. Plain as day. When she came around the rock, Nathan and Daley were hugging each other. There was aren't-we-glad-we're-alive hugging and there was I'm-totally-into-you hugging. And there was no doubt about which one theirs had been.

She and Nathan had talked about it for a while. She knew he was interested in Daley. In fact, it was about all Nathan had talked about lately. Daley this, Daley that. Daley, Daley, Daley. But now it was clear that Daley was interested in him, too.

Nathan always had girlfriends. And it never really bothered her. They were best friends and that was all—nothing romantic between them. But somehow, after seeing Jackson back there with Taylor, the whole thing was really bugging her.

If Jackson was going to hook up with Taylor, and Nathan was like a broken record, talking about Daley all the time—what did that leave Melissa?

Nothing.

From the beginning, the one thing that had gotten her through all the problems they had here was the feeling that she was part of a community. That everybody cared about her. That what she did mattered.

She had worked so hard for this group. Cooking, cleaning, building, listening when people had problems. She'd tried not to complain or bad-mouth anybody. When there were conflicts, she tried to calm everybody down and make everybody happy. And what had she gotten in return? Taken for granted, that's what.

Suddenly Melissa felt alone.

Totally alone.

# NINE

**TWO WEEKS EARLIER**

Abby wasn't sure how long she'd lain there on the floor of the jungle. She didn't feel bad, exactly. She just couldn't move.

Suddenly there was a loud noise, and then something began clattering around her. Like somebody was dropping coins out of the sky. She felt them smacking her skin, landing on her face, her arms, her legs.

*Bizarre,* she thought.

And then she put it together. Thunder. And rain. Huge drops of rain falling straight down on her. Falling on the trees and the banana plant.

*Water,* she thought. *Water. I need to do something about the water.*

But she couldn't quite think what it was she needed to do.

And then the water began running down one of the giant leaves of the banana plant, pouring off the leaf like a fountain. The stream of water was landing right on her face, blinding her. Without any conscious thought, she repositioned her mouth. Suddenly the water was pouring into her.

*Water! I'm drinking water!*

And she was. She was sucking it in, gulping it down. It felt almost like the water was just flowing straight into her veins.

The rain poured and poured and poured. Soon she had drunk as much as she could stand.

After a while, she sat up. She felt stiff and achy, and her mind still seemed vague. But there was something she needed to do, she was sure of it.

Something to do with water. Her brain was so fuzzy. She couldn't think straight.

Then she knew. She had to get water into the bottles. She opened one of the small bottles and positioned it under the stream running off the banana leaf. Amazingly, the rain was coming down so hard that it filled the bottle in seconds. Quickly, she filled the second bottle. That left only the jug. Which had a hole in it.

But if she plugged the hole with her finger, filled it up, then turned it upside down in her pack, the gallon jug would hold its water fine. It took about a minute to fill the jug. She screwed the cap on, then turned it upside down.

The rain continued to pour down on her, soaking her to the skin. She dug around in the pack and pulled out the crackers. They were soaked. But she wolfed them down. Same with the last of the mangoes.

When she was done, she hacked the limb of the banana plant. The bunch of bananas fell at her feet. She stowed them in her pack.

*See?* she thought. *Nature will provide.*

And then, as quickly as it had come, the rain stopped. Within minutes, the sky was clear again, and the jungle sparkled like it was made from a million emeralds. A fairyland.

She hoisted her pack and began walking again. She felt nauseated and shaky, but something inside her told her to keep moving. She got to the top of the next hill . . .

. . . and then her legs abruptly gave out on her. It wasn't like they got weak and wobbly. They just stopped working. She fell in a heap.

*Why can't I stand up?* she thought vaguely.

The answer came to her out of the foggy reaches of the back of her mind. Heatstroke. That's what this was. Even though she had plenty of water in her now, her body would still be catching up for a while. Didn't people go to the hospital for heatstroke sometimes? That was not a comforting thought.

*Maybe I got a little carried away,* she thought. The nausea ebbed and flowed for a while. *Better just lie here for a while.*

Finally the nausea abated a little. Then she felt sleep coming on, like a black curtain falling slowly down around her.

*Just for a while,* she thought. *Just for a little while.*

When Abby woke, it was dark. For a minute she felt terrified, not knowing where she was. There were strange noises around her. She was completely blind. There seemed to be no light at all.

After a while she remembered. *I'm in the jungle. I'm alone.*

She was ravenously hungry. Thirsty, too. She felt around for her pack, drank a whole bottle of water, then ate two bananas.

The effort made her intensely weary. She fell asleep again.

It went on like that for a while. Sleeping, waking up, drinking some water, wolfing down a banana or two, sleeping again.

She wasn't sure how much time went by. At

least a day. Maybe two. Sometimes it was dark. Sometimes light. A voice in the back of her head kept telling her to stand up, to get moving. But she had no strength at all. The dehydration had just flattened her.

Finally she sat up, looked in her pack, and found that the big water jug was nearly empty. And the bananas were gone.

"Abby, you gotta stand up," she said. Her voice sounded odd in her ears. "Abby, stand up."

She stood up.

"Abby," she said, "you gotta start walking."

*Which way?*

"I don't know," she said out loud. "But you gotta go somewhere. Stay here and you'll die."

She picked up the pack and began walking.

Suddenly her mind seemed clear. The jungle around her seemed different now. It wasn't pretty, it wasn't interesting, it wasn't a park, it wasn't millions of emeralds, it wasn't a fairyland. It was the enemy. It was out to kill her.

*Why didn't I understand that before?* she thought.

Nature will provide? What a joke! Nature would provide what you took from it. Otherwise good old Mother Nature would reach out and stomp you like a bug. Nature didn't care about you at all.

# TEN

**THE PRESENT**

## Daley

We've had some close shaves since we landed on this island. If the plane had landed just half a mile in any other direction, we probably would have died. But somehow that was different than what happened with the raft. The plane crash was an accident.

This was something we decided on together. Basically everybody voted to do something that nearly killed us.

The majority thought making a raft was a

good idea. It wasn't. Nathan and I nearly
drowned. Honestly? We *should* have drowned.
If Nathan hadn't been a surfer ... Well, I don't
even like to think about it. The only good thing
we learned is that our system of government
is seriously flawed.

*Hey, we got a great idea. Why don't you guys
go out there and drown!*

It's just not cool.

Oh. Well, I guess there was *one* good thing
about having a brush with death. It makes you
realize what's important.

I told Nathan how I really felt about him. Not
in so many words, maybe. But it was pretty
obvious, huh?

Oops!

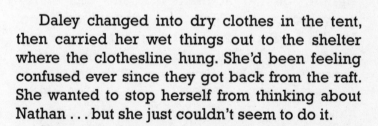

Daley changed into dry clothes in the tent,
then carried her wet things out to the shelter
where the clothesline hung. She'd been feeling
confused ever since they got back from the raft.
She wanted to stop herself from thinking about
Nathan ... but she just couldn't seem to do it.

She went over the same thing that had run
through her mind a zillion times already. Getting
romantic with somebody here was a terrible,
terrible, horrible, dumb idea. Keeping things

on an even keel was hard enough without introducing more complications. If they hooked up, then people would get all bent out of shape about how they were forming a power group so that everybody would have to do what *they* wanted and blah blah blah. It would just add more drama to a situation that had way too much drama as it was.

But still . . . every time she looked at him—

*Okay, okay, okay, Daley,* she thought. *Give it a rest!*

As she started hanging her clothes, she spotted Jackson sitting on the platform with his back against a post, his face pale, while Taylor handed him some water. Daley was a little surprised. Taylor was not the type to help people much—but she'd been really sweet to Jackson while he was recovering from his giardia.

Melissa was sitting on the other side of the shelter, looking at them like she was angry about something. That was kind of odd, too. Maybe Taylor had said something nasty to her or something. Daley couldn't put her finger on it, but the vibe in the camp seemed kind of tense.

Nathan was already at the clothesline, hanging up his wet gear. She felt a surge of excitement as soon as she saw him. Excitement and nervousness.

"Well, that was scary," he said as she approached.

"Yeah, tell me about it," Daley said.

He paused and gave her a significant look. "I'm not talking about the raft," he said.

Daley felt her heartbeat speed up slightly. She raised one eyebrow and met his gaze. "Neither am I."

Nathan frowned and stopped hanging up his clothes. "Okay, I'm really confused."

Daley glanced over toward the shelter. Nobody was paying any attention to them. She leaned forward quickly and gave Nathan a kiss on the cheek. Then she smiled. "Join the club."

Nathan's eyes got wide.

*Okay,* she thought. *Not sure if I should have done that!* She felt embarrassed. And happy. And weird and twisted up and anxious and jumpy and . . . *Oh, man, what am I thinking? Get control of yourself, Daley!*

Abruptly she tossed her wet pants over the line, then turned and walked quickly away.

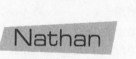

Whoa!

Daley kissed me! Okay, so it was just a kiss on the cheek. But it wasn't like a peck from Aunt Maria. She keeps going on about how we're so wrong for each other, but then . . . she goes and does that.

And this whole thing about how getting together while we're here on the island is a bad idea? Hey, if not here, then where? It's not that I've given up hope of being found—come on!—but we could be here for a while. I don't like thinking that way . . . but it's just a fact. We don't know how long we're gonna be here.

After a while, it's like, *okay, this is my life.* Even though it's a crazy situation, I still get up every day, put my pants on, eat, drink, sleep, whatever. You can't just sit around saying, "Well, everything would be different if I was at home." Sure, that's true. But in the meantime, we gotta live. It's goofy to think you can just keep your feelings on hold forever. If Daley and I have feelings for each other, why deny them? It's hard enough being here as it is— without depriving ourselves of a little bit of companionship.

I *know* she likes me. For a while I wasn't sure. But now I *know.* So I'm not giving up. She'll come around, I'm sure of it.

Melissa had been feeling irritable and out of sorts all day. And the longer the day went on, the worse it got. Every time she turned around, there was Taylor smiling at Jackson or giving him a drink of water or sharing some little joke with him in a low voice so that nobody else could hear.

They weren't holding hands or kissing each other or anything. But it just seemed like something was going on between them.

Finally Melissa couldn't stand it anymore.

She found Taylor folding clothes. She was humming to herself and looked as happy as a clam. Usually work was the one thing that could be guaranteed to put Taylor in a bad mood.

"So. Working, huh?" Melissa said.

Taylor looked up and smiled. She seemed to miss Melissa's uncharacteristic sarcasm. "Yeah, just thought I'd do Jackson's laundry. Poor guy, he's still exhausted from being sick."

Taylor folded one of Jackson's shirts, looked at it skeptically, then refolded it a second time, making it into a perfect square. "There! Perfect!"

Melissa took a deep breath. "Look, I gotta ask you something."

Taylor looked up again. "What?"

Melissa hesitated, then finally just blurted it out. "There's nothing going on between you and Jackson . . ." she said. "Is there?"

Taylor looked like a deer in the headlights, blinking at Melissa. "What! Huh! That's just— Jackson? Me? That's crazy. Why would I . . ." She finally seemed to run out of words.

Melissa felt a rush of happiness at Taylor's denial.

Taylor looked at Melissa for a minute, then her brow furrowed thoughtfully. "Honestly, Melissa?"

Taylor said finally. "I don't know."

Melissa's heart sank.

Taylor looked at Melissa, then swallowed. It only just seemed to be dawning on her that this might be painful to Melissa.

"I . . . uh . . ." Taylor grabbed the stack of clothes. "I better get these back to the tent."

Melissa watched her go. She hated having negative feelings about anybody. But . . . *Taylor*? Did she have to ruin everything? And how could Jackson fall for a such a shallow, vain, spoiled brat? It didn't make any sense at all. It wasn't fair.

As Taylor hurried back toward the tent, she felt something tugging at her brain. Not exactly shame. Taylor rarely got ashamed about anything. But she was feeling a *little* bad.

Anybody could see that Melissa was completely head over heels with Jackson. There'd been a couple of times that Taylor had taken girls' boyfriends away in the past. And she hadn't felt a bit of guilt about it. But this was different. Melissa was—well, you'd have to be a pretty horrible person to want to make her feel bad.

But on the other hand? It was Jackson's choice, wasn't it? If he was digging Melissa, hey, great. But if he wasn't, he wasn't. You can't force it.

The truth was, Taylor and Jackson had some

kind of natural attraction. *It is what it is, right?*

Taylor got to the tent, took the clothes inside, and started folding everything and putting it in neat stacks. When she was done, she thought: *Folding other people's clothes? Me?* She started laughing. *What's wrong with me? Maybe I'm turning into Melissa.*

Then she laughed again. *Nah! Never happen.*

Nathan found Daley frying a fish for supper. He realized he was starving. All that effort swimming to shore after the raft disintegrated really made him hungry.

"How come Melissa's not fixing dinner?" Nathan said. "That's usually her job."

Daley shrugged. "She's been acting really weird today. I don't know what's wrong. I saw her talking to Taylor, and then she kinda stormed off down the beach. I figured if I didn't start cooking, we'd end up hungry tonight."

Nathan looked down at the fish. "Mmm. Smells good."

They stood next to each other for about a minute without speaking. Finally Daley looked up and said, "So . . . what I said to you this morning about being glad you're here is absolutely true."

Nathan was glad she had introduced the subject. Because that was why he'd come over to her. He kind of wanted to pin her down about how she was feeling. "Yeah, and then you kissed me," he said. "Pretty good hug, too, if I remember."

Daley poked the fish, not meeting his eye. "Right. But put it in context. We nearly drowned. It was a total relief just to be alive."

Nathan looked at the fish, sizzling away in the pan, its eye staring blankly up at the sky. He wondered if it would be better to be a fish, just swimming around, gulping down smaller fish and never thinking about anything. "And you kissed me," he said.

Nathan could see her face redden. Hah! He had her now. "You're blushing."

"I am not!" She lowered her head so he couldn't see her face.

"You're gonna fry your face if you get it any closer to that fire," he said.

She looked up at him, flustered. "It was on the cheek! Okay, we're friends. Good friends. This adventure has brought us together, but . . ."

"You kissed me."

Daley looked exasperated. "Nathan . . . I'm sorry if I gave you the wrong impression."

Nathan raised one eyebrow. "Oh! Okay! I get it. So, you're saying you don't think of me as more than a friend."

Daley smiled, looking relieved. "Yes. That's exactly it."

Nathan kept looking at her, smiling in what he hoped was a knowing manner.

"What!" Daley said finally.

"You know what," he said.

Daley glared at him. Or tried to, anyway. He could see right through her, though. "We're friends," she said firmly.

"You're lyyyying," he said, laughing.

"I'm *not!*"

"You're also burning the fish!"

"Aghh!" she said. "Look what you made me do." She raised the stick like she was going to whack him with it.

Nathan danced away from her like a boxer. "Daley's lying, Daley's lying!" he sang.

"About what?" a voice said.

Nathan turned around. It was Melissa, looking at him with a sour expression on her face.

"Nothing, nothing!" Nathan said.

"I was *going* to make the fish, Daley," Melissa said sullenly. "You didn't *have* to do that."

"Sorry," Daley said. "I just thought—"

"No, no, hey, look, whatever." Melissa raised her hands in the air. "Nobody cares how I feel. Why should you be any different?"

She turned and walked away.

"What's her problem?" Daley said.

Nathan shrugged. He knew Melissa. Whatever it was, she'd come around soon. She couldn't stay in a bad mood if she tried.

He danced closer to the fire ring. "Daley's lying," he sang. "Daley's lying!"

Daley had her lips pursed like she was mad. But he could tell she was about to laugh. She brandished the stick again. "If you get any closer, I'm gonna whack you!" she said.

## Daley

Okay, he's right! I do like him. I really do. Big surprise.

But, boy, can he be infuriating.

# ELEVEN

**TEN DAYS EARLIER**

Since the day she'd gotten dehydrated, Abby had been unsuccessful in finding more bananas. It had rained every afternoon, so she had plenty of water. But now she was starving.

Surely some of the plants around here were edible. Problem was, some of them were probably poisonous, too. And she didn't know which was which.

A couple of times she saw a small herd of pigs in the distance rooting under brush. And both times she saw them, the thought crossed her mind that pigs were meat. Meat was food.

Except . . . she was a vegetarian.

When she was a kid, her family didn't eat that

much meat. Her mom was really health conscious. And her dad had some dietary restrictions for religious reasons. But then one day back in middle school, Abby's class had gone on a field trip to a farm up in the Central Valley. The farm had all these sheep and goats and cows. The kids had been allowed to feed the animals.

She had loved the feeling of the cow's lips nuzzling against her hand and the sweet, trusting look in its large brown eyes. She had stroked its flanks through the fence, and the cow had mooed softly at her. As they were driving home, the bus had stopped at a fast food restaurant and suddenly it had just hit her: *I can't eat that.*

How long ago had that juicy hamburger up on the plastic sign been a living, breathing creature? Just like the sweet cow she had been feeding?

And like that, she had decided. No more meat. Not ever. Then she'd started reading about vegetarianism and animal rights and stuff. And the more she read, the more the idea of killing animals for food began to nauseate her.

*Never eat anything with a face.* That was how she'd thought about it. No fish, no chicken, no beef, no nothing.

But now? Out here in the jungle? The thought crossed her mind that maybe she'd been wrong. She started thinking about ways of getting meat. *Maybe I could make a bow and arrow. Maybe I could trick them into falling into a pit. Maybe*

*I could make a net and catch a bird. Maybe I could...*

But then it just seemed impractical. She didn't know how to make a bow and arrow, much less shoot one. Making a net would take days. No, she'd be better off putting her energy into finding more bananas.

Besides, it was wrong.

But by the end of the day, she still hadn't found any bananas.

She came to a stand of bamboo and heard rustling on the far side. Pigs? Monkeys? Some kind of large bird? It was hard to know.

She pulled out her knife and rapidly cut down a piece of bamboo. She felt the pointed edge of the bamboo with her finger. It was as sharp as a razor blade. *It would make a pretty good spear,* she reflected.

She held her breath for a moment, straining to hear whatever animal was on the other side of the bamboo. The animal seemed to have no awareness of her presence. She began creeping slowly through the bushes.

There!

Pigs. There were three of them, a sow and two babies. Her heart began beating hard. It seemed like her vision had begun to narrow, like the pigs were at the far end of a gray tunnel.

*Silently, silently, slowly, slowly,* she thought. *I can do this.*

She continued to creep toward them, holding the sharpened bamboo stake like a javelin. Fifty feet. Forty. Thirty.

The pigs seemed completely unaware of her.

Twenty. Fifteen. If she could just get a few feet closer, maybe she could actually throw the spear and impale the mother pig. She drew her arm back.

*Hold on, Abby!* she thought. *What are you thinking? What has gotten into you?*

She dropped the bamboo pole.

Startled, the pigs whirled around. The mother pig was large and hairy, with short hooked tusks protruding from the sides of her mouth. For a moment she stared at Abby. Her large flat disk of a nose moved, sniffing the air. Her tiny red eyes stared at Abby. They seemed nothing like the eyes of the cow Abby had seen in middle school. They seemed—not exactly evil. But uncaring. Like the pig could have ripped her open with those tusks and wouldn't have cared a bit.

The pig lowered its head slightly. Was it going to charge her?

Abby grabbed the pole off the ground and waved it in the air menacingly. "Get away!" she yelled.

The pig whirled, emitting a blood-curdling high-pitched shriek. And then the pigs disappeared into the underbrush.

Abby stood motionless for a long time, the

bamboo spear clenched in her trembling hands. Could she have done it? She just wasn't sure. *Me? Abby Fujimoto? Hunting?* The whole thing was surreal.

The problem was, she was starving. It was that simple. She frowned. Suddenly something occurred to her. The pigs were eating, right? There must be something edible here.

She looked at the ground and noticed some small green shoots sticking up.

Bamboo shoots. Just like in Chinese cooking. They were eating bamboo shoots!

She ran over to the ground that had been rooted up by the pigs. Most of the bamboo shoots had already been eaten. But there were a few left. She yanked one of them up out of the ground, scraped the dirt off, put it in her mouth, and bit down on it.

It was crunchy. Hey! Not bad!

*What a relief!* She felt a sense of excitement. This was just the start. If she could figure out which other plants were edible . . .

She began hunting around the stand of bamboo, yanking up every bamboo shoot she could find.

She found eleven in about five minutes. But after that, nothing. The pigs had eaten the rest of the bamboo. It was a sobering realization. She was in competition with a bunch of freakin' pigs! And what was worse, right now, the pigs were winning. If they found the food first, she was out of luck. She found herself getting mad at the pigs. They'd stolen her supper! And then on top of that, the mother pig had given her the stink-eye and acted like she was going to attack her. What was up with that!

Abby muttered to herself, complaining about the pigs as she continued to root around, but she found no more bamboo shoots.

Eleven bamboo shoots were enough to stave off hunger. But it wasn't enough to actually make her feel full. In fact . . . she was still starving.

As she was rooting around in the leafy jungle floor—*I'm rooting around like a pig!* she realized—she uncovered a small depression. In the bottom were four large, fat, wriggling grubs.

She stared at them for a long time. She remembered this show she'd seen about these guys in Africa who sold bowls full of these worms at a market. People came up and bought them, then ate them standing there. Like a handful of peanuts.

*Could I really eat those?* she thought, staring at the grubs.

It was more protein than she'd had in days. If she was going to make it out of this jungle, she couldn't afford to be picky. Gross as the whole idea was, she was out of options.

*Never eat anything with a face.*

Did grubs have faces? It was best not to think about it.

"Sorry, guys," she said. Then she scooped them up and tossed all four of them into her mouth.

*"Gross!"* she shouted.

But only after she had swallowed them.

The next morning Abby started recognizing features of the landscape. An unusual outcropping of stone. A strange twisted tree. A volcanic spring that vented a small steaming pool of stinky water that smelled like rotten eggs.

*I've been this way before,* she realized. But not on this trip. She'd been this way when she left camp with Captain Russell and the others.

It occurred to her that she might be able to pick up their trail and follow them from here. She foraged for food as she hiked, eating anything that seemed like it might offer sustenance. Bamboo shoots, grubs, an occasional piece of sour unripe fruit. It was keeping her going. But she knew that she was losing the battle.

It was going to take a lot longer to get to the other side of the island than she'd estimated. She was spending at least half of her time hunting for food. And the hills and the underbrush made the hiking a lot slower than she'd expected. Should she turn around and head back to camp? Everybody would think she was loser, that she'd come slinking back with her tail between her legs because she couldn't hack it out here.

But there was no triumph in starving to death, either.

Just as she was about to turn around, she saw something sticking out of the mud at the bottom of a hill.

A backpack!

She realized that this was where she had gotten separated from Captain Russell and the others a week or so earlier. It had been nighttime in the middle of a huge downpour. She had slipped and dropped her supplies, and then couldn't find the others.

She ran to the pack and tore it open.

*Yes! Food!*

Inside was a whole stack of prepared meals sealed in plastic pouches. She raised her arms and screamed. "Woo-hoo!"

Then she ate two entire meals without stopping.

*Well,* she thought when she was done, *that decides it. I'll push on to the other side of the island. I'll get to the lagoon, and I'll find Captain Russell and the others!*

For the first time since she left the camp, she felt jubilant. Inside the pack was a compass, a small butane stove, a mess kit, a change of clothes—even a toothbrush!

As soon as she had finished eating, she

repacked everything she had brought with her into the larger backpack she'd found on the ground. She looked at the compass. Due north. That would get her right to the lagoon!

It took two days of hard hiking to get to the other side of the island. The problem was that she could never go in a straight line. She was always working her way around obstacles—cliffs, hills, marshes, impassable underbrush—it was always something.

But finally she broke out of the jungle into a grove of palm trees.

And there, on the other side of the trees . . . was the ocean!

It sparkled blue in the bright sunlight, gentle waves rolling onto the shore. Abby ran toward the water.

"Hey! Captain Russell! Jory! Ian! Guys! Hey, I'm here!"

There was no answer.

"Hey! Anybody here? Hello!"

The only sound she heard was the cackling of a group of monkeys back in the trees. In front of her was a long crescent of beach, a perfect natural harbor, protected from the heavy waves. To the east rose the huge, imposing volcano. It was like something out of a movie. She'd never seen anything as beautiful in her life.

Only . . . where *was* everybody? She had been completely convinced they would be here. But it seemed that there was no one here but monkeys. She could see them swinging around in the trees, white-faced little guys with long ringed tails. She laughed briefly at them, then tried to think of what to do next.

Time for a break.

She lowered her pack to the ground. *What a relief!* After hefting the pack for days now, her shoulders were chafed raw and her back was stiff as a board. The water especially weighed the pack down.

She took a quick inventory. There was one meal left. Plenty of water. Just to be on the safe side, she'd been stocking up on food as she hiked. She had enough bamboo shoots, fruit, and berries to last a couple of days.

A plan. She needed a plan. The beach was pretty long. Maybe a mile from end to end. The others could easily be down at the far end. And they'd never hear her.

She decided to leave the pack and jog down the beach. If she didn't find them, she'd head south and hook up with the camp again. She could honestly say that she hadn't found them. She'd given it the old college try, and Captain Russell and the others just weren't there.

Meantime, she'd search the beach carefully to make sure.

She zipped up the pack, leaned it against a tree, and started walking up the beach.

*Freedom!* she thought. Not having the pack on her back made her feel so much better. She walked for about five minutes, calling out occasionally, but receiving no reply. She didn't feel bad, though. She'd done it! She'd set out to reach the far side of the island . . . and by gosh, she'd done it.

Realizing she hadn't had anything even close to a bath in days, she paused to take a quick swim in the ocean. The waves were gentle in the lagoon, and the water was exceptionally clear. She could see sand dollars and shells on the sand below her feet. A school of tiny silver fish flitted past her, their bodies reflecting the sunlight.

After she was finished with her swim, she continued her walk to the end of the beach. She began to feel a little more subdued with each step she took. There was no sign of Captain Russell and the others. No extinguished fire, no litter, no footprints, nothing. When she called out their names, her voice seemed to be swallowed up by the forest.

At the far end of the beach, she found a small sheer cliff. There was no going any farther, so she turned and walked back toward where she'd come from. It was late in the afternoon, and she was starting to get hungry. She thought about the last meal in her pack. Spinach ravioli with cheese sauce. Mmmmm!

The closer she got to her pack, the hungrier she got. She imagined heating it up on the small butane stove in her pack, the smell of the cheese sauce bubbling in her little mess kit. Okay, so she hadn't found Captain Russell and the others. But she had plenty of food to get back to camp. She'd tried, right? Maybe when she got back she could persuade everybody to mount a bigger expedition. Captain Russell and Jory and Ian had to be *somewhere* on the island, right?

She followed her footsteps, saw them heading back into the trees where she'd left her pack. A hundred yards, five minutes of cooking, and she'd be chowing down on that spinach ravioli. Yes!

Monkeys chattered happily back in the trees.

*This isn't so bad at all!* she thought as she crested a small dune and headed toward her pack. The calling of the monkeys grew louder. She'd eat, then she'd sleep on the beach under the stars, then in the morning she'd—

Abby stopped.

Fifty feet away she saw the knot of monkeys. They were bouncing and wriggling comically, clambering over one another, fighting one another for something. Abby laughed.

Suddenly her smile froze. Abby felt her face turn into a mask of fury.

Her pack! The monkeys were climbing all over

*her* pack. She could see all of her things scattered on the jungle floor. Water bottles, clothes, mess kit. A little baby monkey sat off to one side, munching contentedly on one of her bamboo shoots.

"Hey!" she screamed. "Get away from there!"

When they saw her, the monkeys all turned and rose up on their hind legs, fur bristling, baring their needle sharp teeth. Several of the larger monkeys began jumping up and down.

*I'll show you, you little thieves!* She picked up a stick off the ground and ran across the clearing toward the monkeys.

One of the monkeys had the aluminum frying pan in his hand. He whacked it loudly—*bang bang bang bang bang bang bang!*—with her compass. And there was something on his face. Something white and sticky.

"Ai ai ai!" the monkey screeched. It was almost like he was laughing at her.

"Hey! You stupid monkey! You ate my freakin' cheese sauce!" Abby screamed. "I'm gonna kill you!"

The monkeys shrieked and howled as Abby raced toward them. Evidently they weren't used to people, because they weren't as scared of her as they should have been. Abby saw her precious spinach ravioli lying on the ground, cheese sauce soaking into the sandy soil.

She swung her stick at the knot of angry monkeys. "Get away! That's mine!"

The monkeys began retreating, dragging

things with them—bamboo shoots, fruit, her shirt. They weren't really running away, just keeping out of her reach.

The biggest monkey continued to bang on her frying pan with the compass, his eyes wide, teeth bared. "Ai ai ai!" he screeched.

She swung hard with the stick, this time nailing him in the ribs. The monkey squealed in pain and flew backward, cutting a flip in the air.

It was only then that the monkeys seemed to realize what they were up against. They scampered back into the jungle, clambering up trees and howling at her. The big monkey limped away, howling even louder than the rest.

When they got to the tops of the trees, they stared down at her, shouting a chorus of angry cries at her. One of them had something white in its hand.

She gathered up her things. The pack was ripped. The mess kit was scattered. The compass was destroyed. The larger gallon jug of water was unharmed. The two small water bottles had been punctured repeatedly by their tiny teeth, springing leaks and draining into the sand.

And all the food was gone.

"You . . . you . . . you . . . ," she screamed. She couldn't even think of a word bad enough.

The monkeys continued to shower her with abuse. She picked up her frying pan and threw it at the tree. It missed and fell into a bush.

"Just come back down from those trees," she shouted. "Come back here and you're . . . you're *dead meat!*"

Abby dragged the pack back down to the beach and stared out at the blue water. The sun was going down now over the cliff. She had a little water and no food. What was she going to do? There was no bamboo nearby.

She opened the pack again and dumped everything onto the sand. Just in case the monkeys had missed something.

No. There wasn't a scrap of food left.

She was in serious, serious trouble. She took inventory. It was time to stop playing games. She had a knife still. That was good. What else? She saw something gleaming in the sand. Two tiny silver wires. For a moment she thought they were earrings.

But no. As she picked them up, she realized they were fish hooks. Fish hooks attached to a tiny bobbin of fishing line.

She stared at them for a long time.

*Never eat anything with a face.*

Fish have faces.

She laughed loudly, angrily, acridly. So what? Fish have faces? Big deal. Abby Fujimoto had a face, too. Did monkeys care about *her* face when they destroyed all the stuff that kept her alive? Nope. Did pigs care about her face when they ate her food? Nope. Did grubs or fish or birds or anything else out on the island care about the fact that she had a face? Nope. They didn't care if she lived or died.

*The only creature out here who cares about me . . . is me.*

It was all very good and well to sit around in a nice big house in Brentwood talking about how animals had rights, and how all living things were equal. What a crock. Here on the island, things were stripped down to reality. *It's us or them. It's me or you. It's always been that way. I just didn't realize it.*

She calmly threaded the hook onto the line, then went back toward the jungle to find some bait.

An hour later, she was cooking a couple of bony little fish on her butane stove. They sizzled and popped. The smell was intoxicating. *Man!* she thought. *That smells awesome!*

It was the smell of survival.

# TWELVE

**THE PRESENT**

Jackson walked into camp carrying a jug of water. Three days ago, he'd have thought nothing of it. But today, boy, he felt worn out by the time he set it next to the fire ring. He was pooped!

Melissa sat by the fire braiding vines. She looked up as he set down the jug of water.

"Hey," she said tunelessly. She'd been acting weird for a day or so. He couldn't figure out what it was all about. She wasn't her usually bubbly self.

"Hi." Jackson wiped his forehead with the bottom of his shirt. "Man, it's hot!"

"Isn't that Taylor's job?" Melissa said sharply.

"I guess." Jackson picked up a bottle from

the supply of recently boiled water, screwed the cap off, and took a long pull. It really hit the spot. "I've been so useless for the past couple of days, though, I figured I'd give her a hand."

Melissa nodded expressionlessly. Her mouth opened for a moment, like she was about to say something. But then she went back to braiding. Jackson sat down on the sand. He was about out of gas.

Without looking up, Melissa finally spoke. "You like her, don't you?"

"Who?"

"Taylor." Still not looking up.

"Taylor?" Jackson shrugged. Uh-oh. Suddenly he put it all together. He had a hunch he knew where this was going. "Sure. She's all right."

Melissa looked up and threw the braided vine down. "Please don't treat me like an idiot."

"What do you mean?"

"Didn't you tell me it would be wrong to get serious with somebody while we were on the island?"

"Uh . . ." Jackson suddenly wished he was someplace else. "Look, Melissa, Taylor and I aren't any more serious than—"

Melissa was looking straight at him, her expression half hurt, half accusing. "I've seen the two of you together."

Great. She must have seen them when he was sleeping, and Taylor had put her head on his shoulder, and then her hand had sort of dropped on his leg and—"I . . . look . . . come on! This isn't fair," Jackson stammered. He was feeling a little cornered. "We're all just trying to get along with each other. I think we've got a lot more important things to worry about."

He was torn between exhaustion and wanting to get the heck out of this conversation. The whole thing made him feel uncomfortable. *Hey,* he wanted to say, *I don't even know how I feel about Taylor. So how am I supposed to talk to you about it?*

Melissa leaned toward him and her voice dropped. "You know me, Jackson. I'm not somebody who goes around bad-mouthing people all the time. But . . . *Taylor?* You don't know her the way the rest of us do. I bet there aren't five people in our entire class at Hartwell who she hasn't been mean to at one time or other. All she cares about is her hair, her nails, her dresses . . ."

Jackson felt a little defensive. "I know what you see," he said. "I've seen that, too. But honestly, I think there's more to Taylor than meets the eye."

"Yeah." Melissa rolled her eyes. "I know *exactly* what you see."

Jackson folded his arms. "You do, huh? Go ahead. Tell me."

Melissa seemed to deflate. She looked at him wide-eyed, like she was appealing to him. "Jackson! I'm not telling you how to feel. I just want you to be honest."

Jackson liked Melissa. A lot. But things were confusing. How was he supposed to be honest about what he was thinking when it wasn't even straight in his own head? She was right about Taylor. Taylor was vain. Taylor was mean sometimes. But underneath all that stuff, there was a better person struggling to come out.

Or . . . maybe not. How was he supposed to know? People were complicated. You never really knew what was going on in their heads. All he was sure of at this exact second was that he couldn't endure the third degree any longer. What was it with girls? They always wanted to talk, talk, talk. Had talking honestly about your feelings ever changed anything? Jackson doubted it. It just made people get all hurt and angry and weird.

Honest? No, the only thing that would make Melissa happy would be if Jackson told her, *Oh, Melissa, I'm so crazy about you. You're the most beautiful and thoughtful and talented and sweet and perfect girl in the world, and all I think about is you. Let's hop on my white horse and ride off into the sunset!*

But that was totally not happening, bro.

He stood up. "Look, I gotta get some more water."

"Jackson, you're all pale!" Melissa said. "You need to rest. I can help if you—"

He grabbed the empty jug and walked away before she could finish her sentence. *Right now?*

he thought as he trudged wearily back to the well. *Man, this camp is feeling way too small!*

Walking past the fire ring, Daley found Eric busy starting up the fire so that Melissa could cook lunch. Nathan followed her. He'd been following her all day, and it was starting to make her a little antsy.

"We're getting a little low on wood for the fire," Eric said, looking up at them. "Did high tide bring up any new driftwood?"

"I didn't notice," Nathan said. "Did you see any, Daley?"

Daley pointed at the plane, which lay a few feet away on the sand. "You know there's a big old log trapped under the plane. It's probably nice and dry by now. If we could get it out."

She walked over and heaved on the log. It was pretty well wedged under the plane.

"Let me give you a hand," Nathan said. In a joking tone he added, "That's what *friends* are for."

Daley gave him a look. Ever since the conversation they'd had the day before, he had been needling her with stuff like that. She understood where he was coming from. She didn't want to be here any more than he did. If they were at home—hey, she'd get together with him in a skinny minute. But it just wasn't gonna work here. Too many things that could go wrong. Too many things that could get stirred up.

Nathan slid in next to her, grabbing hold of the log. His shoulder touched hers, accidentally-on-purpose.

"Can't do enough for a good *friend*, right?" he said. "And since we're such good *friends*, I'd like to help. But only as a *friend* . . ."

"Nathan, stop!" It just came out of her. She didn't mean to sound quite so harsh. But he was bugging her to death.

Nathan let go of the log, backed up a step or two, and stared at her.

She sighed. Now Daley felt terrible. His big brown eyes were giving her this sad puppy dog look. Which made her even madder. He could look so hurt. Which made her want to . . .

*Okay, not going there.*

"Nathan . . . please! Could you just—" She shook her head. This was going nowhere fast. She turned and started walking swiftly away.

Eric was staring at her. He looked away quickly, like he was embarrassed and started fiddling urgently with the small fire.

"What are you looking at?" she snapped. "And why don't you find your *own* firewood?"

# THIRTEEN

**EIGHT DAYS EARLIER**

For two days, Abby stayed at the beach along the bay, sleeping on the sand. As time went by, she began to gain confidence. In places where she'd found nothing to eat before, she now found food. Roots, berries, leaves, mushrooms—even grubs. She was hungry all the time.

But not starving. There was a big difference!

On her second day at the beach, she found a large dead bird lying near the edge of the jungle. It had long, brightly colored feathers. Her first thought was that it might be worth eating. She ran over, stomach growling. She was disappointed to find that it had been there awhile, so it was too rotten to eat. But then she picked it up and looked at the feathers. They were iridescent greens and reds. And suddenly an idea popped into her head. Feathers!

*Was it possible?* Sure, why not? But first, she needed to find a few more things.

Feeling a sense of purpose and enthusiasm for the first time since she'd found that nobody was here, she went into the jungle and searched for a tree limb. She had a certain shape and size in mind. When she found it, she cut it down and bent it across her knee.

*Perfect!*

She remembered seeing a stand of small bamboo clumps when she was hiking in. They would work. It took her about an hour to find them, but eventually she got there. She was pleased to find that there were plenty of bamboo shoots there. After she had gorged on bamboo shoots, she searched through the stand for the straightest, driest pieces of bamboo she could find. She found ten that she liked, cut them all down, then headed back to the beach.

She took out a long nylon string and the spool of fishing line from her backpack. Then she spent the entire afternoon working.

By the end of the day, she was done. She lifted the tree limb that she'd cut earlier in the day. Attached to it was the nylon cord. She slid one of the thin pieces of bamboo into it, slipped the end of the bamboo onto the nylon cord, and pulled it back. She'd attached feathers to one end of the bamboo with ripstop. On the other end she had attached a small shell, sharpened to a point, with fishing line.

*Beauty!* She'd just made a bow and arrow.

Once she got the hang of it, this would make fishing go a *lot* faster. She could just wade through the shallows until she found fish, then shoot down into the water with the bow. She'd been archery champion three years running at camp back in junior high. This shouldn't be too hard, right?

She set up a target made from a pile of coconut fronds and began practicing.

It didn't work quite like the bows she'd used at camp. But once she got used to it, she was able to shoot fairly accurately. *It's kinda fun, too!*

She waded out into the water and practiced shooting there. She had to compensate for the way light refracted in the water. But after a little practice, she had the hang of it.

A school of fish swam by. She felt a burst of excitement as she drew back the bow and fired.

The excitement turned to irritation, however, as the fish darted away unscathed. She spent another hour or so in the water, growing increasingly frustrated. Okay, fish were a lot harder to hit than she would have thought. If she didn't get a fish soon, she was going to be stuck with nothing but stupid bamboo shoots for supper.

She was about to give up when she heard a

noise from the beach—a loud chattering.

Monkeys!

The monkeys were creeping toward her backpack again. They wanted the bamboo shoots she'd stored there.

"Not this time!" Abby shouted. She charged up out of the surf. The monkeys retreated, howling and jumping up and down. Once again, they seemed to be taunting her.

Without thinking, she drew back the bow and fired at the biggest monkey. The arrow missed narrowly, impaling itself in the sand.

Suddenly she froze. The monkeys froze, too, staring at the bright feathers that were now sticking out of the sand. They'd never seen a bow and arrow before. But it was obvious that somehow they sensed its danger.

Abby swallowed. *I almost shot a monkey!* she thought.

For a moment she wasn't sure quite how she felt about it. Then the big monkey darted forward, grabbed a bamboo shoot from the pack, and ran for the safety of the jungle.

Okay, that was it! Anger surged through her at the thought of spending the night with her stomach knotted up in hunger. When they started stealing her food, the gloves came off!

"I'm gonna kill you!" she shouted. Then she nocked another arrow and started to run after the offending monkey.

The monkey raced for the trees. But it was a small animal, not really made for running. She gained on it as she neared the jungle.

They topped a small dune and then raced for the trees.

Unfortunately, she realized as she plunged through a line of bushes, she had forgotten something. There was a row of sharp volcanic rocks hidden behind the bushes. She tripped and felt something tear in her leg.

Then everything went black.

When she came to, the monkeys were gone. And she knew something was wrong with her ankle.

When she tried to reach for her leg to see how badly she was injured, a sharp pain tore through her arm. She looked down curiously. Something iridescent and green seemed to be poking out of her arm. Her first thought was that it had to be some trick of her eye. Because it wasn't possible that—

It was only then that she realized she had more trouble than just her ankle.

The arrow she had been carrying was now sticking straight through her arm. Her stomach flip-flopped.

*Uh-oh,* she thought. *Now I'm really in trouble.*

Then the world went black again.

# FOURTEEN

**THE PRESENT**

## Nathan

Well, I really screwed up.

Now I think she hates me. I mean, all I want is for us to do what's natural. I like her. She likes me. It's simple as two plus two. But it's like she wants two and two to make five. What's so wrong with *liking* somebody? Huh? Why does it have to be this big deal?

*Oooooh! It's gonna change things!* What's wrong with change? Change is good.

Speaking of which . . .

The whole camp is getting really tense. I don't know what it is. It's like everybody's got some agenda that they're not talking about. We're all going through the motions—gathering food, making the fire, fetching water— but underneath something's not right. Something's changing. And this change . . . well, I know I just said change is good.

But sometimes change is bad.

## Daley

Well, I think I really screwed up.

Now he probably hates me.

I guess I can't even blame him. The thing about Nathan is he always sees the bright side of things. He's like, "Hey, we like each other. Let's get together. What could go wrong?"

Well, a lot. That's the problem.

I mean, he probably hasn't even noticed it. But there's something strange going on around here. Everybody's acting normal. But something's changing. I can't put my finger on it. Everybody just seems like they're backing away from the group.

If Nathan and I got together? Honestly? I think

it might break up the camp. Everybody would be like, "You're just trying to put together a voting block so you can tell us all what to do." Plus Melissa would never admit it, but she's always been a little jealous of his girlfriends. And especially given that she's all into Jackson. And he's obviously not into her.

And is something going on with Taylor and Jackson? I can't tell. All I know is that when you talk to them, it's like they're staring over your shoulder and not even listening to you.

Then there's Eric. Eric's been suspiciously helpful ever since the raft fell apart yesterday. I'm sure he feels bad about almost getting me and Nathan killed. But let's face it, he's always got his own plan. The second he smiles at you, you know he's working on some scheme.

Something's changing.

I'll be the first to admit that change makes me nervous. And I know that change can be a good thing.

But you know what? Sometimes change is bad.

**The next morning after breakfast, Daley was walking down the beach when she saw Nathan**

sitting by himself on the wing of the plane. He was staring out at the ocean with a gloomy expression on his face. She had been hoping for a chance to talk to him. Their last conversation hadn't ended so fabulously.

"Nathan?" she called.

But Nathan didn't answer. He seemed completely absorbed in his thoughts.

She approached him. "Nathan?"

He turned and looked at her without saying anything.

She sat down next to him on the wing of the plane. "I hope you know how tough this is for me."

Nathan looked at her for a minute. "For you? I have no idea what's going on in your head, Daley. I haven't for weeks."

Daley sighed. This was so complicated. The more she shared with him, the closer they'd get. And where would that lead? "I know," she said finally.

"It's like you're two different people," Nathan said. "The bossy, self-righteous Daley I grew up with, and the sincere girl behind that mask. Who am I talking to now? Jekyll or Hyde?"

Daley blanched. It wasn't easy to hear herself described that way. "You're right. I'm handling it badly."

"I don't even know what 'it' is!"

Daley looked out at the ocean. In the distance dark clouds were gathering on the horizon. But it was hard to tell if the storm would hit them or blow right by. "As confusing as everything is here, there are two things I know for sure. One is how much I like you . . . and not just as a friend."

"And what's the other one?" Nathan said.

Daley started to put her hand on his arm. But then she decided not to. "The biggest mistake we could make is to be a couple here. Do you know how scary that would be? I got freaked out just by giving you a kiss on the cheek. We've got to put all our thoughts and energy into surviving. Anything else is just going to make things more complicated."

"How? I don't see it."

"Our little democracy here is kind of on the ropes. You know? Can't you feel it? If we become a couple, even if we don't shove it in anybody's face, it's just gonna make trouble. Every time we vote on something, Eric's gonna say, 'Here we go again! Daley and Nathan vote together on everything.' If Lex votes with us, they'll say we've brainwashed him. If Melissa votes with us, it's because she's your best friend. Eric and Taylor especially will say that they might as well have no vote at all."

Nathan didn't seem all that interested. "Look, whatever. Why don't you just say it? This is a polite blow off, isn't it?"

"No!" Daley said urgently. "Nathan, I've been pushing you away for weeks. I don't want to do that anymore. We need each other. If there's anything I want, it's to have this same conversation with you back at home when things are normal and we can be ourselves."

Nathan stared out at the storm for a long time without speaking. Finally he nodded glumly. "Yeah," he said.

Daley leaned toward him and gave him a hug. For a moment he didn't respond. But then he held her tightly. Daley wished they could do this whenever they wanted. This really was a drag.

It was hard to do . . . but finally she let go.

Nathan took a long breath. "Staying alive on this island is turning out to be much easier than all this personal stuff."

"It's true," Daley said, laughing. She felt so relieved to have everything out in the open now. It finally felt like he understood where she was coming from. "Compared to all this drama, survival is a piece of cake."

"Really?" a voice behind them said.

Daley thought they were alone. Startled, she whipped around to see who it was.

It was Abby. Her face was dirty, scratched, and painfully thin. Her clothes were torn, one arm was stained with dried blood, and her long black hair was a tangled mass. And her left foot was wrapped in rags. She stared at them with an accusing gaze.

"Tell me," she said acidly. "Tell me *exactly* how survival is a piece of cake."

# FIFTEEN

**T**aylor picked up all the aluminum camping dishes after breakfast and started washing them. As a general rule, she tried to avoid anything that might result in her nails getting chipped. But with things going the way they'd been going lately, she was trying to pitch in a little.

Melissa and Jackson had come late and were still sitting on opposite sides of the fire ring, eating. No one had spoken a word since everybody else had left.

"Anybody want some more water?" Taylor said.

She might as well have been talking to a wall.

"Got a couple more pieces of fish here if anybody's still hungry," she added brightly. Lex had gone out early to test a new spear-fishing method he'd come up with, and he had returned with a big haul of fish that looked like red snapper. There was almost a whole fish left over. "Hate to throw it out!"

Still no answer.

Taylor smiled. "Jackson?"

"Nope."

"Melissa?"

Melissa didn't even bother to respond.

Finally Taylor threw down the rag she'd been washing with. "Okay, whatever," she said loudly. "If that's the way it's gonna be, fine. But there's something I want to say."

Jackson and Melissa both turned and looked at her wordlessly.

"I want to say ..." She paused. For a minute she couldn't believe what she was seeing. "Whoa!"

Melissa squinted at her. "Whoa?"

"Look!" Taylor pointed.

They turned and saw Abby limping toward the fire pit, followed by Daley, Nathan, Lex, and Eric. She leaned heavily against a stick that she carried in one hand. A ragged, muddy backpack was slung over her shoulders. *That's not my backpack!* Taylor thought. *What did she do with my pack that she stole from camp weeks ago? Eat it?*

Jackson jumped up. "Hey, wow, Abby! Are you okay? Let me give you a hand."

Abby shrugged him off, not quite slapping his hand . . . but definitely not being Little Miss

Friendly, either. *What's up with that?* Taylor wondered.

"I'm good," Abby said coldly.

Without saying anything else, she walked over to the other side of the pit where a pile of mangoes lay. She began loading the mangoes into her pack. She took the last one and shoved it in her mouth, eating it so fast that the juice ran down her chin.

"Uh . . ." Taylor said. She was tempted to blurt out the party line about everything in the camp being shared equally. But, honestly? Abby was kinda making her nervous. In fact, Abby seemed almost like a completely different person. She used to be the calmest, mellowest person in Hartwell School. Now she looked like a girl who'd been raised by wolves.

Abby, sensing that everyone was staring at her as she took all their food, looked around with a note of challenge in her expression. "Anybody got a problem?"

"No, uh . . . we're just glad you're back," Melissa said.

Abby surveyed the camp, taking in the newly built shelter, the stacks of water jugs, the recently washed shirts and pants and bathing suits hanging on the clothesline. Her lip curled slightly. "You've sure had it easy here," she said.

"Easy?" Taylor said hotly. Abby obviously didn't know what Jackson had gone through. "You don't know what we've had to deal with!"

Abby, who always used to have a smile on her face, looked at Taylor with a flat, empty gaze, almost like she was looking right through Taylor's head. "Really," Abby said, picking up a piece of fish and shoving it in her mouth. "Been pretty rough?"

Taylor couldn't believe it. Abby had been a vegetarian for as long as she could remember. Abby wouldn't even drink milk because she said it was trampling on the rights of cows. It was the only thing that she ever got militant about. Every year she'd gone around the school with a petition trying to get meat banned from the cafeteria, smiling pleasantly at everybody who laughed at her.

"You have no idea," Abby said, licking fish juice off her fingers. "You have no idea how bad it's going to get."

*Gee,* Taylor thought, *what do you say to that?*

Abby looked out at the ocean. "Storm's coming," she said. Then she grabbed the rest of the fish, picking it up by the tail, and hobbled slowly away.

There was a stunned silence.

"Isn't she a vegetarian?" Eric said finally.

"Things change," Jackson said.

# SIXTEEN

**A**fter Abby disappeared, Lex went back to work on his garden. As he was weeding, he thought about what had just happened. It was kind of strange, the way Abby acted. She'd always seemed so nice. But now she was . . . well, frankly, she was scary.

At first he'd thought maybe she'd gone back into the jungle with all those mangoes. But then later he saw her sitting on the edge of the beach, munching away on the fruit. It was like she didn't want to be around the others for some reason.

As Lex was mulling over the morning's events, he heard something rustling in the bushes. He stopped moving. It didn't sound like anything big. But anytime he heard things moving around in the woods, he got a little nervous.

*Scratch scratch scratch.*

He looked around for a stick. Just in case.

*Scratch scratch scratch.* It was closer now. Lex's heart started racing.

Suddenly a white blur came out of the bush. It looked like . . .

Lex's eyes widened. *It was a chicken!*

Lex was sitting so still that the chicken seemed completely oblivious to him. It strutted up and down in front of him, pecking at the ground. It moved strangely, though, like it was injured.

*What do I do?* Lex thought.

There was a cooler sitting next to his leg. Eric had left it there a day or two ago. Suddenly Lex had a burst of inspiration. In one smooth motion, he grabbed the cooler, flipped it over, and plopped it down over the chicken.

"Got you!" he yelled.

Then he stared at the cooler. Inside the cooler, the chicken was clucking and thumping wildly. *Hmm. Now what?* He decided he'd better go talk to Daley, see what she thought.

As lunchtime approached, Daley walked back toward the fire ring with a load of coconuts in her hand. She had to walk a really long way to find them, but they all looked perfectly ripe. As she dumped them next to the fire, Abby came out from behind the plane and walked over to the fire ring without speaking.

Nathan arrived right behind her.

"So, Abby," Nathan said, "you never got a chance to tell us about your adventure."

"Adventure," Abby said. "Yeah. That's one way to put it." Then she said nothing. Instead she started rooting around in their supplies. She pulled out several bottles of water, stuffed them into her pack, then grabbed two of the coconuts that Daley had just spent all morning harvesting.

"Hey, uh, look," Daley said, "everything's been carefully rationed so we all get fair . . ."

Abby gave Daley a steely gaze.

Daley looked at Nathan. Nathan shrugged.

"Okay, whatever," Daley said, raising her hands. "Enjoy."

Daley was about to explain how they had been planning to dry all the mangoes and maybe a couple of the coconuts so that they could store them. Just in case they ran out of food later. But before she had a chance, Lex and Eric ran up.

"Hey, Daley!" Lex said. "You guys gotta see what I—"

Daley held up her hand at him, and he broke off in the middle of his sentence. Melissa and Taylor came out of the tent.

"So Abby, what happened?" Nathan said.

Abby sat heavily on a log, her pack held protectively between her knees. Almost like she was worried somebody might steal it. Slowly, the tension seemed to drain out of her. "Nothing happened."

Melissa stepped over and looked at the cut on Abby's arm. It was deep and infected. "We gotta take care of that, Abby," she said.

Abby pulled away from Melissa.

"I'll get the first-aid kit," Nathan said, running off toward the shelter.

"Did you find Captain Russell and the others?" Melissa asked.

"No," Abby said, standing up. "I'm gonna go wash off."

"You can take a shower," Lex said. "With warm water!"

Abby shook her head disdainfully. "Warm shower. Incredible." She pointed at the pack. "Don't touch my stuff." Then she turned and hobbled toward the ocean.

*Something really bad must have happened out there,* Daley thought. *Otherwise why would she be acting so weird?* It made her feel apprehensive. It was hard to say why . . . but it was almost like Abby had brought some kind of infection into the camp. Daley almost wished she'd go away again. Abby was really kinda creeping her out.

Everybody watched Abby walk down to the shoreline and into the ocean.

In the lull that followed, Lex said, "Hey, everybody. There's something I want to show you."

Lex was excited as he led everybody back to the garden. The chicken raised a lot of interesting questions that didn't have obvious answers.

"Here we are," he said, pointing at the red plastic cooler. He'd put a large rock on top of the cooler so the chicken couldn't get out.

"Wow," Eric said. "A cooler with a rock on top. Once again, I bow to your genius."

"Shut up," Melissa said.

Eric looked at her, surprised. Lex could see what was going through Eric's mind. Melissa was usually the one person he could count on to be nice to everybody when they were being jerks. Eric cocked his head. "Who put the bug up your—"

"Guys!" Jackson said.

Suddenly a frantic thumping noise emitted from the cooler. Everybody jumped back.

"That's not another lizard, is it?" Daley said.

Lex smiled, pushed the heavy rock off the cooler, then put his foot on top. "It's even stranger."

He pulled the cooler rapidly off the chicken. The white chicken looked around, startled. Then it fluffed its wings and began pecking in the dirt.

Everybody laughed.

"That's not strange," Daley said. "It's a chicken."

"It *is* strange," Lex said. "Chickens don't run wild in this part of the world."

"Mmm!" Eric said. "Make mine extra crispy!"

"Eeyew," Taylor said.

"So how did it get here?" Jackson said, scratching his head.

Lex shrugged. "Well, it had to have been brought by people."

"Meaning . . . other people are on the island?"

"I don't know," Lex said. "Kind of a mystery, huh?"

"Why isn't it running away?" Jackson said.

"I think it's hurt."

"So we'd pretty much be doing it a favor to end its misery," Eric said, grinning.

"That's just gross!" Taylor said.

"What? We eat fish!"

"Fish don't have feet."

All the talk about eating the chicken was making Lex uncomfortable. "Look, guys, we're not eating the chicken."

"Why not?" Eric said.

"Because. It's hurt."

Eric rolled his eyes. "Yeah? And . . ."

"What if it lays eggs?" Lex said. "It'd be dumb to get one meal out of the thing if we could have eggs every single day until . . . until we get rescued."

"And what if it's a rooster?" Eric said.

"How many eggs can a chicken lay?" Taylor added.

"A lot!" Lex was starting to feel defensive. It hadn't really occurred to him that anybody would want to eat the chicken. "Four or five a week!"

"That's all?" Eric said. "I say whack it!"

Daley waved her arms. "Hold on, hold on. There's a bigger question here."

"Bigger than food?" Eric stared at her, eyes comically widened.

"Chickens aren't native here," Daley said. "Somebody had to bring it."

"So the question is," Melissa said, "are there more people out there?"

"Or better yet, more chickens?" Eric rubbed his stomach and licked his lips.

"Could you get off that for a minute?" Daley said. "This is serious."

"Hey, I know!" Taylor said. "We could let it go and then follow it to its friends."

"It's a chicken, not a homing pigeon," Lex said.

"I know *exactly* where it's going," Eric said. He took a step toward the bird.

Lex felt a jolt of alarm. It was hard to tell when Eric was joking and when he wasn't. But one thing about Eric, he was always the first guy in line at mealtime. Lex stepped in front of Eric. "No!"

Eric looked at him for a minute. "You didn't . . . uh . . . give this dumb thing a name, did you?"

To Lex's relief, Daley stepped between them. "We're not doing anything until everybody has a say."

"But it's *my* chicken!" Lex said.

"No, seriously, Daley's right," Eric said sarcastically. "There's nothing better than a long, dull, stupid meeting. By the end, you're so brain-dead, you forget you're hungry."

"We'll meet *after* dinner," Daley said. "That way we won't be voting a certain way just because our stomachs are rumbling."

"Great," Eric said. "I can't wait."

"Somebody needs to tell Abby," Daley said. "She's the only one who's not here."

Lex popped the cooler back over the chicken and replaced the rock. As the group split up, something struck him. They had gotten into a pretty comfortable routine here. Everybody pretty much pitched in—even Eric and Taylor—and they pretty much knew what their role was.

But Abby was a stranger to their routine. And she'd come back a very different person from the girl who'd left. There was no telling what might happen now. Lex had a bad feeling that she was about to shake things up.

He waited until everyone had left. Then he moved the cooler behind a bush. Wouldn't hurt to be careful. Not until the whole group had decided what they were going to do.

Afterward, the group broke up and went their separate ways. Melissa and Jackson found themselves walking together down the path toward camp. Melissa had her head down. Jackson wasn't sure if he should say something or not. She was obviously peeved at him.

Before he could think of anything to say, Melissa said, "Look, I'm *not* mad at you."

Jackson looked around, trying to think of a way to phrase what he wanted to say to her. "You've got a right to be mad. What I said before wasn't exactly . . . fair."

"But I get it. This isn't real life. Nothing that happens between us is real."

"It is for now."

They reached the shelter and Melissa sat down on the platform. Jackson sat beside her.

Melissa said, "But we're all doing things we'd never do at home. Would you even look twice at Taylor if you weren't stuck on a tropical island with her?" She hesitated. "No, forget it, don't answer that."

They laughed uncomfortably.

"I mean, no offense, Jackson, but she wouldn't look at *you* twice."

Jackson felt a slight twinge of defensiveness. But the truth was, she was right. "Yeah, I don't even own a Beemer." He thought about the whole thing, trying to put it into perspective. "Here's the thing, Mel. We're here. Whatever happens here, happens here. I honestly don't know how I feel about Taylor. I—"

"Stop it," Melissa said. "Okay? You don't owe me some big candy-coated explanation. Just because I have feelings for you doesn't mean you have to feel the same way."

"But I do."

Melissa's head whipped around. She frowned at him questioningly. "I take it back. I *don't* get it."

"Yeah you do. We're all just scared and looking for a little . . . I don't know . . . security, I guess."

Melissa squinted at him. "So I'm like a security blanket?"

"You're my best friend here!" Jackson said. "But you're Nathan's friend, too. And Nathan is all into Daley. And Taylor can't raise a finger without getting Daley irritated. And Daley's all protective of Lex. It's all totally complicated. It's like a jigsaw puzzle where the pieces keep changing. Things are changing so fast that none of it really matters beyond the minute it happens."

"So then what *does* matter?"

"Finding a way to get home and get back to reality."

# SEVENTEEN

Nathan was sitting at the fire pit when Abby appeared, cleaned up and wearing fresh clothing. Her hair was even combed.

"Wow!" Nathan said. "Look at you! You're almost human again!"

She looked at him without speaking. She was kinda making him nervous. Two weeks ago if you'd made a joke with her, she'd have laughed and spoken to you. Now, it was like she didn't even notice anybody.

Abby rummaged around in one of their storage bins, found the first-aid kit, and began pawing through it, throwing medical supplies on the sand.

"Hey, careful," Nathan cajoled her. "Gotta keep that stuff clean."

Abby looked up at him. "Where's the antiseptic?"

Nathan took the first-aid kit from her and repacked it. "I'll go get it. Eric cut his finger the other day and probably didn't put it back."

He put the first-aid kit back in the bin, then got the antiseptic cream from another bin. "There's clean water over there. You can wash off your arm, then I'll put it on your cut."

He watched Abby as she washed the wound in her arm with water. He hadn't noticed how bad it was. It was more than just a little cut.

He walked over and took her arm. "Here, let me . . ."

She jerked away from him, but then relaxed. Nathan looked more carefully at the wound. It looked like something had gone straight through her arm. Jeez! The skin was all inflamed around it and it was obviously starting to get infected.

"This may hurt," he said. "It's already infected, so I need to work it in there as deep as I can."

"Just do it," she said.

He began rubbing the ointment into her arm. She barely even flinched.

"Does that hurt?" he said.

She looked at him like he was a moron.

"Hey, I'm just trying to help, okay?" Nathan said. "We're not the enemy here."

Abby said nothing as he continued to coat the wound.

"How bad was it out there?" he said finally.

"A lot worse than hanging out here at the resort," she said.

Nathan felt annoyed. She'd called this place a resort two or three times now and it was starting to get on his nerves. He opened his mouth to say something. But then he thought the better of it. What good would it do?

"Hold on," he said. "It's still bleeding a little. Let me get some gauze and bandage it up."

The day seemed to drag by. Every time Daley saw Eric, he gave her a nasty look.

At supper, nobody spoke. They just ate their food and looked glumly at the fire. Daley couldn't help thinking how sick of fish and coconut she had gotten. A nice drumstick would sure taste—

*Stop it!* she thought.

Finally she stood up and said, "Okay, let's start the meeting. Everybody knows about the chicken, right?"

Abby had been eating in silence. She looked up for the first time. "Chicken? What chicken?"

Lex explained about finding the injured chicken at the garden.

"So the question is," Daley continued, "what do we do with it?"

Abby's only response was to walk over by the

plane and start sharpening her knife with a small rock.

"We can't kill it," Lex said. "It's injured. You can't kill an injured creature."

"I don't follow the logic there," Eric said. "Protein's protein."

"If it's a hen, won't we get eggs?"

"Yeah . . . *if*," Eric said. "Who knows how to check?"

"Before we decide about that," Melissa said, "don't we want to figure out where it came from?"

"People could have left a flock here years ago," Eric said. "Captain Cook or some dude like that could have left them here a hundred years go."

"Uh, Captain Cook's voyages in the Pacific were more like two hundred and thirty or forty years ago," Lex said.

"Oh! Sorry!" Eric held up his hands in mock surrender. "My bad. I apologize for being such a totally crappy student of history."

Taylor looked around irritably. "What are we *talking* about here? I don't even know what we're talking about."

"You're right," Eric said. "The bottom line here is when should we fire up the rotisserie?"

"Well, *I'm* not gonna kill it," Taylor said.

"She's right," Nathan said. "We couldn't kill that pig we trapped."

"That was, like, three weeks ago," Eric said. "I'm a lot hungrier now."

"Okay, okay," Daley said. "I think the issue is clear. The fact that the chicken is here doesn't really tell us anything about whether there are other people on the island. Or about when they were here if they're not now. Let's vote. Meat or eggs."

"Meat! Meat! Meat! Meat! Meat!" Eric said, pumping his fists in the air.

He was interrupted by a peal of harsh laughter. Everyone turned to look at Abby, who was still standing over by the plane. She walked toward them, carrying the glittering knife in her hand.

"You people are unbe*liev*able," she said. She waved the knife in a long, slow circle, taking in the vast empty ocean, the long beach, the jungle, the distant mountain. "Does this look like debate club?"

Daley felt her face get hot. "You have something you'd like to add, Abby?" she said coldly.

Abby shoved her knife in the sheath she carried on her belt. "Kill it."

"I thought you were a vegan," Taylor said.

Abby looked at Jackson. "What's with all this voting crap? I thought you were the leader."

"Not anymore," Jackson said.

"I'm the new leader," Daley said.

Abby gave her a surprised look. "Really? I thought everybody hated you."

Daley's jaw tightened.

Before she could speak, though, Nathan cut in. "Hey. That kind of talk may hack it out in the jungle. But not here. Be nice. Daley's the most organized and hardworking person here. We all agreed—*all* of us—that Daley should be in charge."

"Organization? You think that's the most important thing here?" Abby shook her head, looking disgusted.

"As a matter of fact," Daley said hotly, "we've been able to solve a lot of problems by being—"

"Problems?" Abby cut her off. "There's only one problem here. Survival. Kill the chicken. Eat it. Hunt for more."

"Yeah!" Eric said. "Now we're talking!"

"Where's the chicken?" she said. "I'm still hungry."

"It's over by Lex's garden," Eric said.

"No!" Lex said.

Abby pulled out her knife and turned to head up the path that led to Lex's garden.

Before Daley could do anything, Jackson hopped up and stood in front of her. "Wait. I'm not saying you're wrong. But that's not how we do things here."

"You're in my way," Abby said.

Jackson gave her an intimidating stare. "Uh-huh."

Abby's grip tightened on the knife. For a second Daley had the horrible thought that she might lunge at Jackson.

But instead she just stuck the knife back in its sheath and said, "This is stupid."

"It's worked so far," Daley said. "We have plenty of food. We have shelter. We have fire. We have . . . yeah . . . we have a warm shower."

Abby looked at her expressionlessly.

"What about you, Abby?" Daley said. "You have a bad attitude and an infected hole in your arm. So who's the stupid one?"

"You've got food now," Abby said. "And what happens when the seasons change and all those mango trees stop dropping fruit?"

"We'll deal with it then," Daley said.

"Yeah. By sitting here waiting for help that may never come."

There was a long silence at the fire ring. The sun was starting to go down and a cool breeze came off the ocean. Daley shivered.

"Have fun playing government," Abby said. "Then come to me when you get hungry."

She walked off down the beach. Not toward Lex's garden, though, Daley noted.

"Well," Taylor said after Abby was gone, "I guess we know how *she's* gonna vote."

That night Melissa couldn't sleep, so she got up and went out to take a walk on the beach. Moonlight flooded the water, turning the waves silver. Once her eyes adjusted she could see almost as well as in the daytime. Her mind was racing. She couldn't quite put her finger on what was wrong. They had food. Everybody was healthy. But something was wrong. Something beyond her disappointment about how things had gone between her and Jackson.

She noticed a figure crouched under a palm tree. As she got closer, she saw it was Abby.

"You too, huh?" Melissa said.

Abby shrugged. "I'm more comfortable outside."

Melissa sat down next to her. She had never been close friends with Abby—but she had always liked and respected her. They didn't speak for a minute.

"You seem like a different person, Abby," she said finally.

For a moment Abby didn't answer. "I was alone in the jungle twice. And I nearly died both times. The first time I was kind of like, *Oh, you know, it was an accident.* But the second time?" She thought some more. "It's not an accident anymore. Instincts take over, Melissa. Stuff you don't even know is in you. Am I a different person? Not really. It was all there, hiding down inside me. I just didn't know it."

"Hmm."

"Then I come back here and you guys still think you're on a school field trip."

"That's not true."

"Yeah it is. You're all so caught up with who likes who and who's doing more work that you're missing the big picture."

"Which is what?"

Abby pointed out at the ocean. "That right there. The real world. The little fish eat the shrimp, the big fish eat the little fish, the sharks eat the big fish. The strong survive, the weak don't."

"You seem angry."

"Hey, I wish I was sitting around in my house watching a movie on TV and eating Doritos. But that's not happening."

"You'd really kill that chicken?"

"In a heartbeat." She paused. "When I was out there, I ate some grubs. You know how I always used to say I would never eat anything with a face? Well, I was like, do worms have faces? And so I was kinda okay with it. Then these monkeys stole all my food. All I had left were fishhooks. So it was eat fish or die. I ate fish. Then I thought, what if I made a bow and arrow? Then I could shoot monkeys."

Melissa felt surprised. She'd seen monkeys back in the jungle a million times and never even considered that they might eat them. "*Monkeys!* You ate monkeys?"

"Not yet. They're hard to hit."

"Man!" Melissa was quiet for awhile. "You know, the thing is, Abby, that being organized has kept us from *having* to eat monkeys. I mean, I guess I could do it if I was gonna die. But we haven't gotten there. And if we keep working together, we never will."

"Yeah, right."

Melissa's voice got higher. "Why do you say that?"

"Jackson told me today that you guys are traveling farther and farther to find food. Once the fruit season's over, or some little school of fish down there migrates to South America or something, all of a sudden you'll be starving. What's gonna happen then?"

"We'll get organized and—"

"No, you won't."

"I don't see why you say that."

"I bet people have already stolen stuff. Eric? What's he stolen? Food? Medicine? Supplies?"

Melissa was silent.

"All of the above, huh?"

"That's Eric. He's just one person."

"Things haven't even gotten bad here. You just wait. When there's no next meal, your cute little organization will fall apart. I mean . . . it's already happening! Look around you. All the petty little jealousies, the backbiting, the factions . . ." She shook her head. "It's just a matter of time, Melissa.

Eventually it's every man for himself. The strong survive, the weak get eaten."

"I think you're just saying this stuff because you're scared. I know the real Abby. You didn't bring your bow and arrow into camp, did you? You left it somewhere out in the jungle so we wouldn't see it."

Abby shrugged. "So?"

"You were embarrassed, weren't you? You thought we'd think it was funny—Abby the vegan turned into this big meat-eating hunter."

Abby looked calmly out at the sea. After a few seconds, she laughed—a brief dismissive snort. "You're so naive, Melissa."

"Why do you say that?"

"I left my bow and arrow in the woods so nobody would steal it."

The whole conversation was scaring Melissa. It made her feel so bad that her stomach hurt. "Look, Abby, I'm going back in the shelter where it's comfortable," she said. "You should, too."

# EIGHTEEN

The next morning, Lex went to check on the chicken. He had poked some holes in the cooler so that it could breathe. He was worried about its injury. With all the hoopla yesterday about everybody wanting to eat the chicken, he'd never had a chance to examine it and find out what was wrong with it.

As he popped the top of the cooler off, he was surprised to see that the chicken had fashioned a small nest out of leaves and sticks under the cooler.

"So what's hurt?" he said. "Is it your leg? Can you fly? I'm gonna take care of you . . ."

The chicken saw a small bug in the dirt, lunged for it, and gobbled it down. As it did so, it exposed the center of the nest. In the middle of the nest was . . .

"An egg!" Lex shouted. "Look at you, you crazy chicken! You laid an egg." He scooped up the egg.

"You know what, chicken," he said, "the best thing I can do for your health is to go back and show this to everybody. Then I'll come back and try to figure out what's wrong with you."

Abby took the splint off her ankle at the fire pit after breakfast. The swelling was starting to come down a little. Nathan sat at the fire pit watching her.

"That splint was pretty smart," he said.

Abby couldn't figure out quite what it was— but everything the Happy Campers said seemed to irritate her. "I didn't have a choice."

"You know the only reason we've done so well is because we've taken care of each other."

"So I've heard," Abby said. "About ten times now. But the fact is, I'm alive because I took care of myself."

To Abby's annoyance, Nathan looked like he was ready to engage in more debate club. Fortunately he was interrupted.

"Hey! Hey!" It was Daley's kid brother, running up to the fire pit holding something in the air. "Look! We've got an egg. This proves it's a hen!"

Hearing the noise, Eric and Taylor came out of the shelter.

"Wow," Eric said. "A whole egg. Let's not all fight over it."

"Should we keep it till it lays more?" Nathan said.

"No," Lex said. "We should eat it before it goes bad."

"So who gets it?" Taylor said.

"Let's vote," Nathan said. "Maybe one person eats it, then every time there's a new egg . . ."

Abby couldn't stand listening to this tripe any more. Voting, sharing, talking, blah blah blah. It made her sick! She stood up and grabbed the egg.

"Good," Abby said. "I'm first. You can vote about the next one."

"Hey!" Taylor said. "That's not fair."

Abby took out her knife, chopped the top off the egg, and sucked it down raw. It was better than grubs, that was for sure.

"Ohhhhh!" Eric said. "Check her *out*! That is just awesome! Abby, you're my hero."

Abby glared at him. She wasn't out to be anybody's freakin' hero. She just wanted to eat. She'd probably lost fifteen pounds out in the woods. And she needed to gain it back.

Nathan looked at her sternly. "That's not how we do things around here," he said.

"Not yet," Abby said.

She looked around the fire ring. There was nothing left to eat. There was a big stand of bamboo outside camp. As far as she could tell, the Happy Campers hadn't discovered that you could eat bamboo shoots. She figured she'd go get some. Before they figured out the secret and ate them all.

Eric

Man, I thought I'd died and gone to heaven. Abby grabbed that egg and just totally scarfed it down. Raw, dude! Raw! You should have seen the look on Nathan's face. It was like his perfect little world of rules and regulations was just—*pkkeaaaaoowwwww!* Down in flames, man.

Finally! Finally, somebody besides me has the guts to call them on all this democracy and voting crap. Things are gonna be different. I can feel it!

An hour or so later Eric found Abby down the beach near the big stand of bamboo. He was hoping he'd find her. He saw that she was munching on something. As soon as she heard him coming, she stuffed her food into her backpack so he couldn't see it.

"What are you eating?" he said.

"Nothing," she said stonily.

"Loved the thing with the egg this morning,"

he said. "Nathan about had a cow."

Abby just sat there looking at him.

Eric gave her a confidential grin. "Yeah, it's gonna be great having somebody else around who doesn't give in to the pressure."

Abby's hand rested on the handle of her knife. Like she was about ready to defend herself from evildoers. She was cool . . . but she seemed a little jumpy. A little paranoid.

"So how's the ankle?"

"What do you want, Eric?"

Jeez, she made it hard to have a conversation, though. He plopped down next to her on the sand. "Same thing you do."

"What's that?"

He held up one finger. "One. I want to stay alive." He lifted a second finger. "Two. I want to get off this crappy, hot, bug-infested, miserable island."

"Doesn't everybody?"

"In theory? Sure, I guess. But the way they're doing it? Daley and Nathan especially? I don't know. I don't think they're serious about it. They're so bogged down in chore lists and stuff, they've lost sight of the main goal. We get out of here, we survive. We stay . . . " He shrugged. "Who knows."

"I thought you were all one big happy family."

"Yeah, right. There're two camps here. One

camp wants to dig in and play house. The others are ready to get active." He leaned toward her. "I see you being someone who wants a little action."

"Where do you stand?" Abby said.

Eric spread his hands. "Me? Come on!" He laughed. "Me, I want some chicken."

Eric was gratified to see a tiny smile appear at the corners of her mouth.

"Think about it," he said.

Jackson arrived at the shelter with a load of coconuts. He dumped them on the ground, then wiped his forehead. Taylor came out with some water.

"Thirsty?" she said.

He nodded. "Big time."

She handed him the bottle of water. He drained it. It was warm—almost verging on being hot. Boy, he was tired of drinking hot water. For a moment he imagined being home, sipping on a nice cold soda, the ice clinking around in the glass, the water dripping off the sides, the—

"Jackson?" Taylor said. Her brow was furrowed and she looked troubled.

"You okay?"

"Sure." She took the empty bottle from him and put it with the pile of empties that needed to be washed. Then she looked up at him again.

"So, does Abby give you the creeps?"

Jackson shrugged. He'd known people back in the 'hood who sometimes seemed like Abby. Desperate, scared, unpredictable, hungry for something . . . Some of them had even been friends of his. "A little," he said. "She's been through a lot."

"We've *all* been through a lot," Taylor said. "But we didn't turn into . . . cave people."

Jackson laughed softly and sat down. Taylor sat down next to him. He was conscious of the fact that she was sitting a lot closer to him than she would have a week or so ago. It was a subtle thing . . . but a clear sign that something was different between them.

She must have sensed it, too, because she said, "Even more confusing, what's going on here?" She waved her hand at the inch or two of air that separated their bodies. "I mean, with us?"

"*Is* something going on?" he said.

"Oh, give me a break!" she said.

Jackson sighed. Why couldn't this stuff be simpler? "After we crashed," he said finally, "things were pretty clear. Fire, water, food, shelter. Everything else was just static. But lately, things are getting . . . confusing."

Taylor made a face. "Are we talking about Melissa here?"

"Sort of." Jackson said. "But it's more than just . . . relationships."

"So what is it?" she said impatiently.

Jackson thought about it. He looked over at her. Even without makeup and fancy dresses and everything, she was a really beautiful girl. Sometimes it was hard to think straight in front of a girl like that. Melissa was a cute girl, too. And yet he wasn't all that attracted to her. What was up with that? Maybe he just didn't really go for sane girls. That was kind of a depressing thought.

Finally he said, "I'm still trying to figure that out."

Taylor stood and smoothed out the front of her dress. "Tell me when you do?"

Jackson nodded.

## Jackson

Now what?

I mean—Taylor's definitely digging me. That's obvious. And I'm feeling something for her, too. What is it, though? I feel like if I had any sense, I'd be all into Melissa. She's the nicest person here. She's generous, she's sweet, she's diligent. She never argues over stupid stuff. She's totally crazy about me. And she's actually really pretty, too, if you get past that meek little thing she's got going.

And yet. I don't know. It's like, every time I sit down next to Taylor and talk to her, I feel . . . I feel better. I feel good. *Really* good.

So, like I said: *Now what?* Here we are out in the middle of nowhere. No rules, no limits, no parents, no nothing. We can do anything we want.

Which, honestly, is kinda scary.

# NINETEEN

**D**aley was sitting by the side of the path to Lex's garden when Abby marched by, her knife in her hand. Abby didn't speak to Daley, didn't even meet her eye. It was a little spooky.

"Hey!" Daley called. "Wait! What are you doing?"

"Guess," Abby said.

Daley jumped up and ran after her. At first Daley had been willing to give Abby a little slack about eating all the food that wasn't nailed down. After all, she'd come out of the woods looking like she'd about starved to death. But now the whole take-everybody-else's-stuff routine was starting to get under Daley's skin. "You're not killing that chicken," Daley said firmly.

"I'm not?" Abby stared straight ahead, walking

as briskly down the path as her injured ankle would allow.

"Abby, it might come to that. But not until we all vote on what to do."

Abby stopped short, turned, and gave Daley a hard stare. Her black eyes seemed empty. "You really don't get it, do you?"

"What?"

"You think survival is about rules."

"It's worked so far."

"Wake up, Daley! We're all one breath away from disaster. One storm. One accident. One injury, and all this Happy Camper teamwork and good sportsmanship nonsense is done for. Your democracy can't stop disasters."

"But it helps. Everybody thinks so."

"Really?" Abby rolled her eyes. "Maybe you don't know your . . . *family* as well as you think."

"What does that mean?"

"It means some of us want to eat chicken." She smiled without warmth. "And we will, majority or not."

Then she started walking down the path again.

"Abby! Abby, listen to me!" Daley followed her. But Abby didn't stop until she reached the garden. "Stop!" Desperately Daley called out, "Everybody! Help!"

Lex looked up and saw Abby walking toward the chicken. He had made a small pen for it to live in. As Abby approached the pen, Lex threw himself in front of her.

"Get out of my way, Lex," Abby said. She still had the knife in her hand.

Daley felt a rush of anger. "Don't you dare touch my brother!" she shouted.

Abby shot her a look. "Gimme a break, Daley," she said. Then she turned to Lex. In a soft, calm voice she said, "Lex, it's not a pet."

Lex looked agonized. "But it's hurt! You have to take care of something that's hurt. Like we're trying to take care of you!"

Abby blinked and didn't move.

Nathan and Eric ran into the clearing. "What's going on?" Nathan shouted.

Abby turned to Nathan and said, "I'm going to kill the chicken." Her voice seemed unnaturally calm.

"No!" Daley said, grabbing the wrist with which Abby held the knife. "This isn't how we do things."

Abby shook her hand off. "You people keep saying that. What is wrong with you? You're like a bunch of freakin' robots."

Jackson trotted into the clearing.

"Let's just calm down. Abby, we know you had a rough time in the jungle. But that wasn't our fault. You seem like you're mad at us because of a choice *you* made."

"You say it like it's my fault."

Daley jumped in. "Wasn't it?" she said sharply. "You're the one who wanted to go off on your own. We all said, 'Don't do it. It's dangerous. There's nobody to help you.' And what did you do? You ignored us."

Abby's jaw clenched and her eyes blazed.

Before she could say anything though, Nathan said. "Hey, hey, hey, hold on. That's history. You're right, Abby. Compared to what you went through, we've got it easy here."

"You have no idea what I went through!"

"Okay, but whatever it was, it would have been better if you'd had somebody to help you. Abby, you've got people here who'll help you. But it can't just be a one-way street, we give and you take."

Suddenly Eric blurted out, "Would you leave her alone!" Normally Eric's bluster seemed calculated. But this time, he seemed genuinely emotional about something. "If she wants chicken, she should have chicken . . . so long as she shares."

Daley said, "Look, Abby, we can't stop you. But if you kill that chicken, you're saying you don't want to be one of us. Do you really want to be on your own again? Out there eating . . . bugs and tree roots and stuff?"

Abby didn't move. Her hands were trembling and her cheeks were flushed.

Finally someone spoke. It was Jackson. "Wait,"

he said, stepping forward. "I'm not sure I agree with you, Daley."

"What?" Daley said. "What do you mean?"

"I think maybe it's time for a change," he said.

"What kind of change?" Nathan demanded.

Jackson held up his hands. "Let's just cool down, all right?" He looked at Abby. "All right?"

Abby stared back at Jackson.

"Leave the chicken alone, Abby," he said.

She continued to stare at him. Finally, though, her shoulders twitched slightly. She turned to Daley and said, "Okay. You think you're a strong enough leader to keep us alive, Daley?" She took her knife out and held it out between two fingers.

Daley stared silently at the knife. It was razor sharp, the edge glittering in Daley's hand.

"Prove it, Daley," Abby said. "We're hungry."

Daley felt like she was being put on the spot. She had no intention of killing the chicken. But she wasn't going to sit here and let Abby challenge her without responding. She reached out and, took the knife, held it out at arm's length.

Daley's eyes met Abby's. Daley looked for something in there that she could communicate with. What had happened to the softness, the sweetness that had been there before? Daley couldn't see it. It was like black curtains had been pulled down inside her eyes.

Suddenly Abby turned and walked away.

"I'll get the fire going!" Eric said, following

Abby as she walked away. They headed down the path back toward the camp.

"No!" Daley called. "We're doing this the right way. Who wants me to kill the chicken?"

She looked around the circle of faces. She was still holding the knife out like it might bite her.

To her intense relief, nobody raised their hand.

"Good," Daley said. "Four say no. That's a majority."

"Except there's eight of us now," Jackson said.

"Then let's say it's four to four," Daley said. "I'm the leader. I break the tie." She flung the knife on the ground. Everybody looked down at it nervously. "I say the chicken lives."

For a moment her mind felt settled. But then she remembered what Jackson had just said— that it was time for a change. Was he suggesting that her leadership wasn't any good?

Daley turned to Jackson. "And what kind of change are you talking about, anyway?" she demanded.

Jackson looked thoughtful for a minute, then he frowned. "I'm not even sure myself," he said.

Then he turned and walked away from the campsite, leaving Daley standing there with Nathan and Lex. Lex bent over and picked up the knife. Daley gave Nathan a worried look.

"I don't know," Nathan said.

"Are you saying you think Jackson's right?"

she said. "Are you saying we need a change?

He shrugged. "I don't know."

Daley felt a stab of frustration. "You don't know . . . *what*?"

Nathan shrugged again. "I don't know," he said. "I don't know what I don't know."

Daley shook her hands in the air. "Aghhhh!" she shouted.

# TWENTY

The next morning, Taylor was sitting at the campsite braiding vines for a new kind of fishnet that Lex had designed. Melissa had been sitting across from her for half an hour without speaking once. Taylor had tried a bunch of conversation starters—the weather, food, the confrontation between Daley and Abby—but nothing worked. Melissa just sat there like a lump.

Taylor felt like she was going to explode.

"Enough!" Taylor finally shouted. "We can't keep icing each other like this."

Melissa just kept braiding the vines in her hand. She didn't even look up.

"I don't know how long we're going to be stuck here, but if we don't talk, it'll feel like a lifetime."

Melissa's jaw clenched. "There's nothing to talk about," she whispered.

Taylor was sick of this. She dropped her vines on the ground, walked over, and sat with her knees almost touching Melissa's. She was going to make Melissa look at her if it killed her!

"I'm sorry that Jackson and I have . . . connected," Taylor said, trying not to sound mad. And, hey, she *was* sorry. It wasn't like she was setting out to make Melissa feel bad. But you can't help how you feel. Right? "I know how much you like him . . ."

Melissa cut her off. "It doesn't matter to me how you two feel about each other," she said.

Taylor wasn't sure if she was being sarcastic or not. "Oh," she said. "Then I guess we don't have a problem."

For the first time, Melissa looked up at her. Her eyes were wet. "What matters is that you knew how I felt, and it didn't stop you from trying to get close to him."

"But I didn't try!" Taylor spluttered. "It just . . . I just . . . it was . . ."

Melissa's eyes narrowed. "You're so full of your own baloney that you actually believe that. Don't you?"

Taylor's eyes widened. What was she *talking* about?

Melissa looked at her for a long time. "You're a selfish, devious person, Taylor," she said finally. "I don't trust you anymore."

Taylor felt her face whiten. How could Melissa

say something so . . . mean? "Melissa! That's just not fair!"

"Fair?" Melissa said. "Tell me about it."

Melissa stood and walked away, leaving her half-braided vine lying on the sand. Taylor thought about running after her. But what good would it do? It was obvious Melissa wasn't going to change her mind anytime soon.

Eric spotted Abby sitting on the wing of the plane, rubbing her injured ankle with a wet bandana. It wasn't totally obvious what he should say to her. The New Abby—as he was starting to think of her—was a little touchy. And right now he didn't want to get on her bad side. When he first got here, he'd thought that he had found an ally in Taylor. But now he was thinking he'd been wrong. The thing about Taylor was that she was flighty. You couldn't really count on her to think one thing or another.

At the moment she seemed to be totally under Jackson's spell.

So he was going to have to find another ally. He figured Abby might be the one.

Eric approached her with a serious look on his face. He was pretty sure that his usual jokey approach wasn't going to hack it. "Hey," he said. "How's the ankle?"

Abby looked up at him. Her face wasn't showing any pain. But the ankle looked pretty banged up. Eric felt a knot in his stomach just looking at it. "I can walk," she said.

Eric nodded and looked away from the ankle. Best to change the subject, anyway. He figured dwelling on her injuries wouldn't get him anywhere. "So . . ." he said. "What's next?"

She looked at him curiously. "Next? Next for whom? What are you talking about?"

Eric cleared his throat. "Well, obviously you don't buy into Daley's little democracy thing. It's getting pretty tense around here."

Abby shrugged. "So?"

Talking to her was like talking to a wall. She just didn't seem to grasp all the issues. Or maybe she didn't care. "Well, you know . . . it seems like what we've got going here is not working so great. So . . . I'm trying to kind of weigh my options. You know what I mean?"

Abby looked out at the ocean. It was obvious that she didn't care squat about his options. He tried to think of a way to phrase things that would make her see that maybe they were both in the same boat.

Before he could think of anything, though, Abby spoke. "I'm thinking maybe the others might have gone west."

Eric was a little shocked. Beat up as she was, it sounded like she wanted to . . . "So are you saying what I think you're saying?" Eric said. "You actually want to go out . . ." He pointed at the jungle. "Are you saying you actually want to go *out there* again?"

"I'd rather be looking for help than waiting for disaster."

Eric took a deep breath. Now was his chance! "Take me with you," he said.

Abby frowned. "What?"

Eric felt excited for the first time since the group had agreed to test out his raft idea. "Sitting around is driving me *crazy!*" he said. "I want to do something to get home. Maybe we can . . . I don't know . . . find out where that chicken is from."

One corner of Abby's lips twisted into a disdainful smile. "You?"

"What!"

"Eric, you wouldn't last two minutes out there."

Eric was tempted to disagree with her. But the truth was, she was probably right. He wasn't exactly Mr. Rough-and-Ready. "Okay, Abby, you're right. You've got all the experience. But together we'd make it. And maybe we'd find the others, too!"

Abby looked him up and down. It was obvious she didn't think much of what she saw. "Eric, you're just as clueless as the rest of them."

Eric was finally starting to get annoyed. "Clueless?" He laughed derisively. "You want to

talk about clueless? You're the one who nearly
died out there. Twice. Want to try for a third?
*That's* clueless."

Abby's face was impassive as ever.

"Dude, you really want to find the others?" he
said. "I'm all you got."

After a moment a line formed just over Abby's
nose. She looked at the jungle thoughtfully.
"Hmm," she said.

"Listen," he said. "I've got an idea . . ."

## Eric

Just had a very, very, very interesting talk with
Abby. As usual, it took me a while to convince
her that I was serious. But I think she gets it
now.

Sometimes when you're going to start a
movement, you need an idea guy. I mean, okay,
I'm not the world's best guy at executing
things. But ideas? Yeah, I can think up new
ideas.

So today Abby and I talked. And I think we're
gonna get something going here.

All this time, I've been one guy. One guy fighting
six people. And I'm not the world's most
popular guy, either. But now I've got Abby on
my side. I think with two people, I can turn the

corner and make something happen.

I'm not the only one here who's tired of the Daley 'n Nathan Happy Homemaker Show. It's just a question of prying a couple more people loose.

And now, with Abby's help, I'm sure I can do it.

Finally!

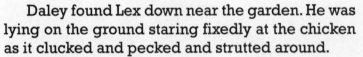

Daley found Lex down near the garden. He was lying on the ground staring fixedly at the chicken as it clucked and pecked and strutted around.

"Lunchtime, Lex," she said.

He didn't seem to notice she was there. He frowned at the chicken.

"Come on, Lex," Daley said. "It's time for lunch."

He looked up as though he had just noticed she was there. "No, I'm okay," he said.

Daley sat down beside him. "The chicken's safe, Lex. Nobody's going to touch it now. We voted."

Lex continued to watch the bird. "No," he said finally, "I'm not worried about that. I'm just kinda studying the chicken. It's amazing the stuff you can learn if you just look at something for a long time."

"You need to get something to eat," Daley said.

Lex sat up and chewed on his lip for a minute. "What happened, Daley?" he said finally.

"What do you mean?"

"We were doing so well. Now I feel like we're crashing again."

"There're always going to be disagreements. That's why the democracy is so important. But it's working, and we're fine."

Lex smiled at her. "You think?"

"Sure," she said. "Come on. Let's get some food. I promise, we're fine."

## Daley

Are we really fine? I don't know.

Part of me wants to say that it's just a passing thing. When we've got an emergency—like when the plane got washed away and we had to pull it ashore again, or when Lex got lost in the woods—it gives us something to focus on. But when everything's going pretty well—like it is right now—everybody starts looking around for ways to mess everything up. What's the old saying? Idle hands are the devil's workshop?

Well, the point is once people get some time on their hands, they start getting into mischief. Especially Eric! But honestly, right now Eric's not the main problem. It's Abby that's really throwing us for a loop. She just seems to have a different agenda than the rest of us.

And I don't understand it.

I mean, to me she seems . . . crazy. I don't know how else to say it. Twice she's gone out there and twice she's nearly died. And what's she got to show for it? Has she found Captain Russell and the other kids? Nope. Has she found evidence that anybody else is living on the island? Nope. Has she found new sources of food, new tools, a better place to live, something we can use to signal for help? Nope. She's accomplished absolutely zip.

All she's got to show for it is a gash in her arm, a sprained ankle, and a bad attitude.

So what I don't understand is why people seem to actually be listening to her! Every time she talks, it's like half the kids in the group are nodding their heads like she's saying something that makes sense. Jackson, Eric, sometimes even Taylor.

It seems like if she said, "Hey, let's all go jump off a cliff," some of the kids would actually nod their heads and go, "Hmm, that's a very interesting idea."

Are we all going nuts? I don't get it! I'm scared.

At the end of lunch, Eric stood up and said, "Okay, is everybody listening?"

The group stopped talking. Everybody looked at him.

He grinned. "I know this is gonna come as a shock to everybody. But Abby and I are actually gonna do it."

Everybody stared at him.

"Do *what*?" Taylor said finally.

"The unthinkable!" Eric was having fun, dragging it all out.

"Yeah, yeah, yeah," Nathan said.

"We're . . ."

Eric kept looking around grinning, letting the suspense build.

"Eric!" Daley said in her usual Mama Bear tone. "Just spit it out."

"We're . . ." Eric held up his hands solemnly. "We're . . . calling a *meeting*!"

# TWENTY-ONE

**M**elissa found Jackson sitting in the clearing next to the shelter, bashing coconuts on a rock. The coconuts had a thick green husk that had to be knocked off before you could get to the hard inner shell. It was hard work, and most of the time nobody wanted to do it. Jackson's face had a grim expression as he whacked the coconuts methodically into the rock.

Jackson didn't speak as she sat down opposite him. He just grunted rhythmically as he worked.

"So what do you think of this meeting that Eric and Abby called?" she said.

Jackson said nothing.

"I mean, why wouldn't they say what it was about? All Eric would say was that it was a 'big surprise.'"

Jackson didn't look like he cared one way or the other. He just kept thumping the coconuts on the rock. A pile of green husks covered the ground around his feet. Just a few days ago, Melissa had felt like she could tell him anything. And that he would tell her things he wouldn't tell any of the other kids. Now it was like she had no idea what he was thinking.

"Daley says you've been acting strange," Melissa said. "If I did anything to . . ."

"It's not you, Mel."

"Then what is it?" Melissa asked.

Jackson lifted a coconut high in the air and brought it down with a crash on the rock. It barely even dented the coconut. He looked at the coconut and grimaced. "Is this it?" he said. "Are we looking at the rest of our lives here? Smashing coconuts and playing mind games?"

Under her breath Melissa muttered, "And not knowing who you can trust?"

She wasn't sure if he heard her or not. He shot her a questioning look. But she didn't respond to him.

"Rescue is going to come, Jackson," she said firmly.

"Yeah, well, the wait is starting to get to me," he said. Then he smashed the coconut on the rock again. The husk split this time. A piece flew off and hit Jackson in the face, leaving a small scrape on his cheek.

"This isn't 1800," Melissa said. "Planes and boats go everywhere. Maybe it'll take another couple of weeks. Maybe another month. Maybe two. Who knows. But we will get rescued."

Jackson held his fingers to his face and looked at the small smear of blood that came away on his finger. He frowned, then looked back at Melissa. "Look," he said, holding up his finger, showing her the dime-size red smear. "This little scrape is nothing. But what if it gets infected? What if I get sepsis or blood poisoning or some freaky flesh-eating virus? I'm not saying it's gonna happen. It's just that every piddly little thing that happens is an opportunity for disaster."

"Sure, but . . ."

He looked intently at her. "Melissa, I could have died just three days ago. Something like that happens, suddenly you start seeing the world a little differently. I'm just not feeling all patient and optimistic right now."

"What's the alternative?"

"I don't know. But where's the urgency in our little democracy here? The answer to every problem is, 'Let's sit around and talk about it.' It's time to *do* something." He picked up another coconut and whacked it on the rock. The husk tore off cleanly.

She threw up her hands. "What are we gonna do? Make an airplane out of vines and driftwood? We can't even make a boat."

"I don't know. All I know is that I've had it with talking."

Melissa felt a chill run through her. What could she even say to that? No matter what she said, Jackson would just think it was more pointless talk.

Finally she stood up and walked away.

After Melissa walked away, Jackson finished husking the coconuts. God, he was sick of this kind of drudgery!

He thought back to a month ago when he'd first found out that he was going to be able to go on the trip to Palau. It had sounded like paradise. He'd spent his entire life in Los Angeles. Other than the occasional school field trip? As far he could recall, he'd never even left the city limits.

Beaches and cute girls and interesting animals. The whole thing had sounded like a dream come true. And now it had come down to this. Working like a fry cook at some burger joint, just trying to stay alive.

There had to be a better way! There just had to be. He wondered what this meeting was going to be about tonight. Maybe it would be a chance to shake things up. Because whacking on coconuts all day was getting pretty stale.

As he was gathering up the coconuts he'd

husked, he heard a noise behind him.

Startled, he whipped around.

But it was just Abby, kind of staring at him with this odd look on her face.

"What?" he said.

She shrugged. "Didn't mean to scare you."

He continued to gather coconuts, stacking them in a pile. Abby made no move to help him. It irritated him a little.

"You know," she said finally, "you're still the leader here."

"Actually, I believe that would be Daley's job description," he said.

"But you're the one they rely on."

Jackson wasn't sure if this was true or not. Maybe in some ways it was. But that was the last thing he wanted, people looking at him all the time with this goony expression—like they thought he was going to solve all their problems.

When Jackson didn't respond to her, Abby said, "You're not happy here."

"Is anybody?"

"I don't know," Abby said. "Daley and Nathan seem pretty comfortable. I mean, I know they want to get home and everything. But they still seem to think this is some kind of little Junior Achievement project." She put a fake little happy smile on her face. "Say, kids! Let's go off into the woods and see who can survive on a can of baked beans and a box of coconuts! Winner gets an extra special merit badge and a free pass to Harvard!"

Jackson shrugged. She had a point.

"You're torn," she said. "Aren't you?"

"About what?"

"Come on. Don't play dumb. About whether it's best to hang out here and try to make sure everybody's okay . . . or whether it's best to take action to get home."

Jackson sighed loudly. She'd struck a nerve. This was pretty much exactly what he'd been wrestling with when she'd appeared out of the woods.

"You seem more like the kind of guy who wants to take action," she said.

"Yeah," he said. "But what kind of action?"

She smiled. "I've got some ideas . . ." she said.

Nathan, Daley, and Lex were walking out to the garden. Lex claimed he had discovered something unique and fascinating about chicken behavior that he wanted to show to them. Daley wasn't all that interested . . . but sometimes you had to indulge Lex a little, just to make him feel better.

"What kind of surprise could Eric and Abby possibly have for us?" Daley said.

"I know!" Nathan said, grinning. "They're going to apologize for all the grief they've ever given us."

"Oh, of course!" Daley said. "Then it'll snow and we'll all go ice skating."

They all laughed.

"Poor old Abby's in such a strange state of mind," Nathan said. "I bet Eric's roped her into another one of his goofy schemes."

"Maybe he's got a new boat design," Lex said.

"All I've got to say is I'm never getting on any kind of transportation device designed by that guy again!" Daley said.

Nathan held out his fist and they rapped knuckles.

Things had been a little uncomfortable between her and Nathan for a day or two there. But now it seemed like they were settling back into a nice groove again.

"What's with Eric, anyway?" Nathan said. "He's not dumb. But it's like every idea he has falls apart once it comes time to execute."

"Remember the house he tried to build?" Lex said. "He spent all day working on it, then he barely breathed on it and the whole thing fell down."

They laughed again.

"Or his fire-starting device? The thing with the mirror?" Nathan said. "It seemed like an okay idea, concentrating sunlight into one little point ... but he just couldn't make it work."

They shook their heads sadly.

"He's always got to find a shortcut," Daley said. "He just doesn't understand that getting things done requires a lot of tedious work."

"Yeah," Nathan said, "he says he wants to change things, he wants to do things his own way, he wants this, he wants that . . . but he's just not willing to—"

Suddenly Lex interrupted their conversation with a loud scream. "No!"

"What!" Daley shouted, her heart suddenly pounding.

Lex pointed wordlessly. In front of them was the chicken coop that he'd made the previous day.

"She's gone!" he shouted. "She's gone!"

Daley ran to the chicken coop. Lex was right. The chicken coop was empty.

"Maybe she escaped," Daley said.

Lex rattled the cage, checking to see if anything had come loose. But the cage was solidly constructed from slats of bamboo. Nothing seemed loose and there were no holes in the sides.

"No way!" Lex said frantically. "She's hurt. She couldn't have gotten out of here."

Nathan and Daley exchanged glances. It was obvious they were thinking the same things. Was this the "surprise" that Abby and Eric had in mind for them? Were they going to show up at dinner with a bunch of drumsticks?

"They took her!" Lex shouted. Daley hadn't seen Lex this angry before in a long time. Maybe not ever. His hands were trembling and his face was white. "They're gonna kill her!"

# TWENTY-TWO

"They can't do this!" Lex wailed. "We voted!" He began looking through the bushes around the chicken coop.

"Maybe it's not too late," Daley said.

Nathan nodded. "We better go check back at camp."

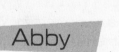

Abby

Eric is an idiot. No, that's not right. He's not an idiot. But he's naive. He doesn't really understand how harsh things are here.

Still, the thing about Eric is he's not afraid to

think of something new. I mean, I have a lot
of respect for Daley and Nathan. You stick
them in an American high school with lots
of food and water and cars and clothes and
books and computers and stuff ... and they're
impressive kids. That's their element, you
know? You get up, you go to school, you go
to tennis practice or yearbook staff, you ride
home in your dad's expensive car, you do your
homework ... hey, Daley and Nathan are the
queen and king of that stuff.

Everything's predictable and safe.
Everything's tried and true. Ivy Leagues, here
we come.

But here? Forget it! You can try to make a
routine. You can try to make a safe little space
where everything's predictable. But it's a
waste of time.

Here nothing will ever be predictable. Nothing
will ever be safe.

Get used to it.

Whatever you want to say about Eric, he
understands this. And Nathan and Daley?
Totally clueless.

So we kind of come down to a choice here.
Do we just whistle past the graveyard with
Nathan and Daley? Do we play along with
their little "democracy"? Or do we have the
courage to do the right thing—the *smart*

thing—even though it's going to make them mad?

Sorry, guys, no hard feelings. But I'm not taking a bullet for the team here. This isn't about winning the popularity contest or getting voted president of the junior class.

This is about survival.

And the thing I learned out there in the woods is that when it comes to survival, I'm gonna do whatever it takes.

What*ever* it takes.

As he approached camp, Nathan found Jackson and Abby walking toward the fire ring, each carrying an armload of coconuts. Nathan was not in the mood to be nice. They'd voted and Abby had lost fair and square. And then she thought she was going to walk off and do her own thing? It was totally not cool.

"Hey!" Nathan shouted at her. "Where is it?" Abby looked at him blankly. "Where's what?"

Nathan was used to Eric playing stupid. But when Abby did it—it made him furious. "Don't give me that," he said angrily.

Abby's eyes narrowed. Her hand slid down her side to the butt of her knife. *Okay,* Nathan thought, *that is a little creepy.* What was she going to do—pull a knife on him?

"What are you talking about?" she said.

"You gonna tell me you haven't been out at Lex's garden this afternoon?" Nathan shouted.

She raised her chin slightly and cocked her head, her hand tightening around the knife. "Why? What's it to you?"

"She's been with me all afternoon," Jackson said. He put his hand on Abby's arm. "What's going on?"

"*All* afternoon?" Nathan said.

"For the past couple of hours, yeah," Jackson said.

Nathan looked at Jackson, then at Abby, then at Jackson again. One thing he felt pretty sure of—you could trust Jackson to mean what he said. Nathan wasn't always sure what was going on in the guy's head. But Jackson never lied about anything.

"You can chill out with the knife, Abby," Nathan said. "We're not in the 'hood here."

"No," she said. "This is a lot worse."

Nathan rolled his eyes. Then it hit him. Of course. If Abby were going to take the chicken, she'd have just done it. She wouldn't have been sneaky about it. The only person who'd be sneaky was . . .

"Eric," Nathan muttered.

"What about Eric?" Abby said.

"Forget it," Nathan said. Then he began running again.

Nathan only had to search for a few more

minutes. He found Eric sitting at the fire ring munching away on something. It figured! It totally figured. Nathan stopped short. He couldn't believe it. Eric was being so brazen about it—just sitting there munching away like it was no big thing.

Suddenly Nathan felt a wave of hunger sweep through him. Chicken! Oh, man! Nathan realized that not only was he peeved at Eric for killing the chicken, but he was angry because ... well, on top of stealing the chicken, Eric was hogging it for himself. Nathan's mouth watered as he watched Eric chewing happily away in front of the fire.

He remembered, with a certain amount of bitterness, the last time he'd been to KFC. He could almost taste the chicken thigh he'd eaten. The crunchy outside, the hot steaming—

*Okay, okay, that's enough dwelling on the past,* Nathan thought. Then his eyes fixed on Eric again.

"You're unbelievable!" Nathan said disgustedly, approaching the fire ring.

Eric looked up innocently, his mouth stuffed with food. He smirked. "Thank you very much," he said, a couple of tiny bits of food spraying out of his mouth. "Why?"

"You had to do it, didn't you?" Nathan looked around for evidence. And halfway hoping there might be a piece left that *he* could eat. There was nothing. Eric hadn't left a shred of evidence, not even the bones.

"Huh?" Eric's eyes were wide. He blinked. "Had

to do what?"

Nathan stalked around the fire, picked up a stick, and poked at it. "Did you throw them in the fire? Huh? Probably left half the meat on them, too."

Eric's lip curled. "Dude, I don't know what you're whining about. But I'm tired of hearing it." He stood up and tossed something into the fire and then started to walk away.

Nathan tried to fish out whatever it was that Eric had tossed into the fire. But it was too hot.

"Burning the evidence?" Nathan called. "You're such a coward!"

Eric continued to walk away.

"Don't you walk away from me!" Nathan called. Nathan hadn't felt so furious in a long time. A whole chicken! Eric had eaten an entire chicken in one sitting! And not shared a single bit of it? It was just about the lowest thing Eric had ever done. First Eric had nearly gotten him killed. And now he was eating everybody else's food? Suddenly it was like he was seeing Eric through a red haze.

"Waaa waaa waaaaaa!" Eric said over his shoulder. "I am so done with you."

Nathan hadn't felt this mad in ages. The anger rolled through him like a tide. "I don't *think* so!"

Without even thinking, Nathan hurled himself at Eric. Hearing the rush of footsteps behind him, Eric turned. But he was too late. Nathan's shoulder caught Eric just under the ribs. A perfect tackle, just like Coach Renfro had taught him in football. *WHAM!* Eric went down with a grunt.

Nathan expected Eric to fold up. But instead, as Nathan fell on top of the smaller boy, Eric began squirming and spinning. Nathan grabbed his arms. He wasn't quite sure what he was going to do when he subdued Eric—punch him? Shake him? Dump sand in his mouth?—but Eric didn't give him much of a chance. Eric started bucking and kicking and shaking like a bag full of rats. Nathan was amazed at how hard Eric was to control.

"What are you doing, man?" Eric shouted. "Hey! Somebody! Help!"

Nathan grabbed one of Eric's wrists and forced it down on the sand. Eric continued to struggle. For a guy who always complained about how weak he was and how bad his back was and all that crap, Eric was actually pretty strong.

"Help! What'd I do? Help!"

"You know *exactly* what you did," Nathan hissed. He could see pieces of food in Eric's mouth. The sight of it made him even angrier.

Then the other kids began running out of the woods.

"What's going on?" Daley called anxiously.

"He's gone crazy!" Eric yelled. "Get him off of me!"

"Nathan, calm down!" Taylor called.

"Help! Help! I didn't do anything."

"Yeah," Nathan said. Now he had control of Eric's other wrist. He pushed his face down so he was looking straight into Eric's eyes. "You didn't do anything at all. Did you?"

"Help!"

Jackson ran toward them and grabbed hold of Nathan's shoulders. "Stop," he said firmly. "It's over."

But Nathan was so angry that even Jackson couldn't hold him back.

"You didn't do anything, huh?" Nathan said, staring straight into Eric's startled eyes. "Nothing except kill the chicken."

Jackson continued to pull on his shoulders. Finally he managed to raise Nathan off of Eric's chest. As Nathan tried to shrug off Jackson's grip, he saw Melissa coming out of the woods.

In her arms was—

"Oops!" Nathan whispered, suddenly feeling all the anger drain out of him.

And Melissa? Melissa was holding . . .

The chicken.

# TWENTY-THREE

**A** few minutes later, Melissa was helping Lex put the chicken back in the pen. Now that she had found out why Nathan had attacked Eric, she felt terrible.

"I'm sorry," she said. "It was all alone. I was afraid Abby might do something."

"It was my fault," Lex said. "I shouldn't have left."

Daley had come along with them. "It's everybody's fault," she said.

"How's that?" Melissa said.

"We don't trust each other anymore," Daley said.

Nathan wandered off by himself, very

embarrassed at what he had done. *God,* he thought. *What a total idiot!*

It had turned out that Eric was just eating a mango. And the thing he'd thrown into the fire had been a mango pit. If he had bothered to look at Eric instead of just jumping on him, he'd have seen that Eric was eating something orange. It didn't even look vaguely like chicken. But Nathan had gotten so mad that he'd only seen what he'd wanted to see.

And what he'd wanted to see was Eric stealing the chicken.

Nathan walked down the beach for a while, finally stopped, sat down on a piece of driftwood, and stared out at the water. The waves were still breaking out on the sandbar, massive curls of water, just like in one of those videos about crazy big-wave surfers. He could hardly believe that he had survived out there.

"Don't feel bad," a voice behind him said.

He looked up and saw Abby standing behind him. He looked away, feeling completely humiliated. "Tell me why not," he said. "Please."

"This isn't home," Abby said breezily. "We can't always do the polite, practical thing."

"I don't buy that." Nathan picked up a shell and threw it into the ocean. "Just because we're alone doesn't mean we have to get all primitive."

"Nice theory," she said. "But wrong."

"Oh?"

She shrugged. "Hey, if there's anything I learned out there in the jungle, it's that it's the primitive parts of us that will get us out of here. All that be-nice goody-goody stuff we've been taught all our lives? Useless out there. I actually let a bunch of monkeys steal my food one time. I was like, 'Oh, they're so cute and funny!' But you know what? They're not. Behind those cute little fuzzy faces, all they were thinking about when they saw me was: *How can we steal that big funny-looking monkey's food?*"

"I don't see your point."

"We're just monkeys, Nathan. We're big, smart monkeys. When the chips are down, we're no different from them. You just start thinking, *Me or them?* You don't think, *Oh, I'm a vegan.* You don't think, *Golly, they're just cute little monkeys.* You don't think about whether they're on the endangered species list. All you think about is who's going to survive."

Nathan felt a panicky sensation. What if she was right?

But no . . . no, she couldn't be.

"Things were going so well," he said wistfully. "Until . . ."

Abby laughed. "Until I came back?" Nathan didn't say anything. It was what he meant. But he didn't want to say it. He glanced at Abby for a minute. She didn't look offended. In fact, she didn't seem emotional one way or the other. Not happy, not sad, not angry. She could have been talking about the weather.

"I'm not the problem, Nathan," she said.

"I don't mean this personally," he said. "But I think you are."

She scratched her nose and looked out at the big waves. "You remember that story about Sir Isaac Newton and the apple? He was sitting under a tree and this apple fell on his head. It made him think about gravity. Next thing he knew, he had come up with a mathematical explanation for gravity."

"And?"

"Suppose he'd just eaten the apple."

"Huh?"

"Gravity's still gravity. Whether you believe in it or not, gravity's there. Whether you have a scientific explanation for it or not, gravity's there. Whether you've got an apple in your hand or not, gravity's still there."

"Uh . . ."

"I'm just the apple, Nathan," she said. She made a sweeping gesture with her arm, taking in the ocean, the island, the sky, everything. "The ocean that keeps trying to drown us, the storms that blow our stuff away, the germs in the water that make us sick, the monkeys that steal our food—all that stuff is gravity. You can believe in it or not. But you can't stop it."

Nathan wasn't sure how to even respond. She

had sounded so certain about everything. For the first day or so she'd seemed angry. But now she seemed calm—like the old Abby. Except that in the new Abby, everything the old Abby believed in had been turned upside down. It made him feel scared. Not of her.

But what if . . .

What if she was right? "So what's this meeting going to be about?" Nathan said.

Abby didn't answer.

"Come on, Abby," Nathan said.

"You'll find out," she said.

Nathan sat there waiting for her to say something else. But she just looked expressionlessly out at the ocean. He found himself getting angrier and angrier at her.

Finally he got up and walked away in disgust.

"I'm just the apple," she called.

*I'm just the apple?* What did that even mean?

Jackson sat on an upturned plastic container. The one they usually stored their safe drinking water in. Only today, nobody seemed to have gotten around to boiling more water.

After a while, Taylor came over and sat across from him.

"We've been here three weeks," Taylor said

in a small, girlish voice, "and I've never been so scared."

"Don't be," Jackson said. "You're with friends. They'll always be here for you." He tried to sound convincing. But he wasn't completely sure he believed it.

"Are you one of them?" she said. "Will you always be here?"

*Here we go again,* Jackson thought. *Another girl conversation.* "Yeah, I'm your friend. Of course. But I want to do what's best. For everybody."

She looked at him with irritation. "What's that even mean?"

Jackson didn't answer.

"And what's this meeting going to be about?" Taylor said. "The one that Eric and Abby called?"

"We've all got some thinking to do," Jackson said.

"About *what*?" Taylor sounded angry now. "It's like everybody's been talking in riddles for the past three or four days."

"We can't think for one another. Everybody's on their own."

Taylor grabbed his arm like she was trying to keep from getting swept away in an ocean current. "What are you *talking* about, Jackson?"

Jackson shook his head. "I'm not even sure I know."

"But it's something to do with this meeting," she said. "Isn't it?"

Jackson sighed loudly. "Yeah," he said. "Yeah, it is."

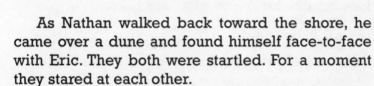

As Nathan walked back toward the shore, he came over a dune and found himself face-to-face with Eric. They both were startled. For a moment they stared at each other.

"It's just about supper time, isn't it?" Nathan asked.

Eric eyed Nathan apprehensively. "Yeah," he said.

"Time for the big meeting, huh? The big surprise?"

Eric nodded. For once he didn't have his usual sneaky expression on his face. If anything, he looked worried.

Without saying anything, they started walking back toward the camp. A small plume of smoke rose from the distant fire.

"I'm sorry, man," Nathan said after they'd walked silently beside each other for a while. "I lost it."

Eric looked at Nathan for a moment, then shrugged. "Hey, you know what? I'm not even mad."

"You should be."

Eric smiled thinly. "Truth? I'm kinda glad it happened. It just proved my point."

Nathan looked curiously at Eric. "Which is?"

"The whole time I've been here I've been feeling like maybe there was something wrong with me. You and Daley seem so . . . certain. And Jackson, you know, he just kinda stands there looking like he knows what he's doing."

"Okay."

"This whole time I've been feeling like you and Daley were just plain wrong. But every time I tried to say it, you guys made me feel like a moron."

"I don't think that's what we were—"

"That's not the point. Who cares what you intended? Or me either, for that matter. This isn't about hurting somebody's feelings or patting somebody on the back. The only thing that counts is this: There are two different ways of thinking going on here."

"Look, Abby's been through a lot, but—"

Eric gave Nathan a look out of the corner of his eye. "Can you just let me finish, dude?"

"Sorry."

"There are two ways of thinking here. It's not just a passing thing. It's not like everybody who disagrees with you is gonna wake up tomorrow and go, 'Whoa, I was totally wrong! What was I thinking?'"

Nathan considered what Eric was saying for a minute. He'd been trying to tell himself that that was exactly what was going to happen, that after a while everything would blow over and go back to normal. But Eric was right. There was a real split in the camp. And it wasn't going to heal up overnight.

"Nathan," Eric said, "only one of us can be right."

They were approaching the camp now. Nathan could see Daley and Melissa busily working away around the campfire.

"So what do we do about it?" Nathan said.

Eric smiled mysteriously. "We make the problem go away." Then Eric began running toward the camp.

Nathan's heart began beating rapidly all of a sudden, as though something bad were about to happen. But what? *I'm being irrational,* Nathan thought. They had plenty of food, plenty of water, decent shelter. Things were moving in the right direction. What could possibly go wrong? So they'd had some disagreements. Big deal. Eric was always making mountains out of molehills. People always had disagreements. That was human nature. But they'd resolve them just like they always had. They'd discuss things, they'd vote, they'd move on.

Right?

Nathan watched as Eric reached camp, picked up a pan and a wooden spoon, and started banging on the pan. "Camp meeting!" he yelled. "Time for the camp meeting!"

And for a moment, Nathan felt the strangest urge . . .

. . . to turn around and run away.

# TWENTY-FOUR

"**C**amp meeting!" Eric called again. "Camp meeting!"

Daley saw that everyone had finally arrived. Abby seemed calm and determined, of course. Nathan sat beside her with an apprehensive look on his face. Taylor, too, looked nervous. Lex seemed agitated, and Melissa kept looking at the ground. Even Jackson, whose face normally seemed so unreadable, looked a little uncomfortable. The only person who looked enthusiastic was Eric.

Eric finally quieted down. For a moment there was silence—no sound but the wind and the dull crash of the waves.

"So what's the big announcement?" Daley said.

Eric and Abby exchanged glances. Eric gave her a brief nod, then she stood up and looked around the group.

"I've caused a lot of problems since I came back," Abby said. "I'm sorry for that. But I truly believe we can't survive here forever."

"We won't have to," Daley said. "Rescue is coming."

Abby made a slightly impatient face. "We don't know that for sure." She paused. "That's why I'm leaving again tomorrow."

Daley felt her eyes widen. She looked at Nathan. Nathan shook his head sadly, like he couldn't believe she was doing something so dangerous and crazy.

"I'm going to explore the west side of the island," Abby said.

"You can't!" It came out of Daley's mouth before she could stop herself.

"Yeah, I can," Abby said calmly. "Maybe the others went that way, maybe there's a weather station, who knows? The only thing that's clear to me is I don't fit in here anymore."

"But you already went over there!" Nathan said.

"There's a small bay over there. That's all I looked at. There's a ton of territory over there that I didn't even look at."

"Look, Abby, I know it's been a little rough settling in here," Nathan said. "We've gotten sort of settled about how we do some stuff. And maybe we haven't done such a hot job at helping you adapt, but—"

"That's not the point. You want to be here playing house or camping or hunkering down or whatever you want to call it . . . and I don't. I'm going. That's final."

"You can't!" Taylor said. "We're not going to let you die out there all by yourself!"

"She's not going to be alone," Eric said.

Everyone looked at him, puzzled. Then it started to sink in, what he was talking about.

"What!" Melissa said.

"You can't be serious!" Daley said.

"You?" Nathan said. "Out there humping it through the boonies? Eating worms and stuff? That's not the Eric I know."

"Yup!" Eric said with a smile. "We're going to find out where that chicken came from!"

There was a long silence. Daley felt like something was building inside her, something that was about to burst.

"No!" she said finally. "Forget it!"

Eric stared at her, blinked once, then a second time. "Huh?" he said finally.

"You can't go," Daley said firmly. She realized that it was time to put her foot down. Everybody was getting all irrational. It was like a fever sweeping through the camp. Somebody had to stop this nonsense before something really bad happened. "Nobody can go."

Abby looked at her with an even gaze. "It's not your call, Daley."

"I know that!" Daley said hotly. She was getting sick of this silliness. "It's *our* call. All of us. We *all* decide. That's what we agreed on, right?"

She looked around the group expecting everyone to nod in agreement. Jackson looked out at the water. Melissa was looking at the ground, drawing little designs in the sand with her toe.

"No," Eric said. "That's what you forced on us."

Daley was starting to feel mad now. How could people be so *stupid*? "Eric! No! C'mon," she said. "We've been doing so well. Sure, there're problems. But we're surviving. Abby says we won't . . . but look around us. We've built shelter, made fire, located water and food. It's only going to get better, more comfortable, more liveable . . . until we get found."

"I don't care," Eric said. "I can't stand this any longer."

"We're surviving!" Daley said again. "The democracy is what keeps us going! Melissa? Am I wrong?"

Melissa looked up uncertainly. "No, I mean, sure, I guess you're right. But . . ."

"But what?" Daley threw up her arms. "We're proof it works. We're here! We're alive!"

"But . . ." Melissa looked at the ground again. "For how much longer?"

Daley was starting to feel desperate now. She felt like the boy with the finger in the dyke, leaks springing all around her. "Don't say that! It's not perfect. But it's kept us alive. We got the plane up out of the water, we've got water and—"

"You keep saying that same stuff," Eric said. His voice was high and urgent. "And I keep saying that it's not good enough. But do you listen? No, you don't."

There was a long pause.

Finally Nathan spoke. "Daley?"

She turned and looked at him. There was something in his eyes that made her think he was about to sell her out. Her jaw hardened.

"You said it yourself," he said softly. "A democracy only works if everybody wants it to work." He spread his hands helplessly. "Right now . . . not everybody does."

Daley felt like everything was falling apart. She wasn't sure if she was going to cry or scream. "But most do!" she said desperately. "That's what it's all about! The majority. I'll prove it. We'll vote. Who thinks we should all take a breath, calm down, and stay together? Hands up!"

She raised her hand and looked at around the circle.

Nobody even moved.

"Melissa?" she said. "Nathan! Come on! I know you guys think this is crazy."

"Going into the bush?" Nathan said. "Yeah, I think that's crazy. But—"

Daley ignored him. "Me, Nathan, Melissa, that's

three. Taylor? Lex? You guys know this is nuts. That's five, right?" Nobody was actually raising their hands. But she felt sure they all agreed with her. "We all want to stay together except Eric and Abby! Right?"

The surf thundered against the beach.

Finally someone spoke. "No."

She turned and saw that it was Jackson. The first word he'd said since the meeting started.

"What!" she said.

"No." Jackson said it again. Jackson looked at Daley with a calm expression in his eyes. "I've always gone along with the group, even when I didn't agree," he said. "It's worked till now. Fine. But you know what? I'm tired of waiting. So it's time for something new."

Jackson stood up, walked across the fire pit, and sat down next to Eric and Abby.

"So," Jackson said, "I'm going with Eric and Abby."

# TWENTY-FIVE

**T**he next morning Lex stood next to Daley, watching as Jackson took down the tent and packed it into his backpack. Soon Eric and Abby joined him.

"I should help," Daley said. Lex saw her wiping away tears.

Lex took her hand. "Let them do it," he said. "It's their decision."

Daley sighed. "Yeah, I guess. I just feel so . . . responsible."

"They'll be okay," Lex said. "They're a lot better prepared than Abby was. They've got more food, more water. They've got shelter."

Nathan and Taylor came up and joined Lex and Daley. They both looked sad.

Eric looked up from his work, "Come on, guys!" he said. "You saw this coming, didn't you?"

He frowned. "I mean . . . *didn't* you?"

Nobody answered. Lex wasn't sure if he'd seen it coming or not. He was pretty sure Nathan and Daley hadn't. They'd been so wrapped up in everything here, they couldn't see past their own feelings.

"I'm not a jerk!" Eric said. He grinned. "At least not all the time. But I'm not going crazy here."

Suddenly Taylor ran forward and threw her arms around him. Eric blinked, looking a little stunned, his hands hanging in midair. Then, finally, he grabbed her and hugged her back. Lex was surprised to see that Taylor looked like she was about to cry.

"Don't be long, all right?" Taylor said.

Eric nodded, then pulled away from her. "If there's something out there, we'll find it."

Impulsively Lex grabbed the fire-starter that Eric had designed a week or so earlier and thrust it into Eric's hands. "We can make another one," he said.

Eric smiled and hesitantly accepted the fire-starter, a metal cone with a mirrored interior surface. He looked like he was about to turn away, but then he reached forward and tousled Lex's hair. "Take care of everybody, okay genius?"

Lex nodded seriously. After all the times that Eric had been mean to him, it was kind of nice to see that he could be decent, too.

"Let me grab some water for you," Nathan

said, picking up a heavy jug of water and stowing it in Abby's pack.

There was now a row of packs lined up against the log where they sat at the fire pit. Jackson shouldered his pack, then looked around. "All set?" he said to Abby and Eric.

Abby and Eric grabbed their packs, too.

"Let's do it," Eric said.

Lex frowned. There was something odd going on. He hadn't noticed it earlier, but there was a fourth pack, fully loaded, propped against the log. "Wait!" Lex said. "You've got too many packs."

Daley and Nathan looked curiously at the fourth pack.

Then a voice said, "No, they don't."

Lex turned to see who it was. Melissa stood at the edge of the clearing. She wore her hiking boots and a broad hat. *This is puzzling!* Lex thought.

"Huh?" Nathan said.

"I'm going, too," Melissa said quietly.

"What!" Nathan said.

"No!" Daley sounded shocked.

Taylor could only say, "But, but, but . . ."

Lex turned and looked at Abby, Eric, and Jackson. It was clear from their faces that they already knew.

"We've always said how we're stronger as a group," Melissa said, walking toward them. "Now we need to keep two groups strong."

Nathan put his hand on her arm. "Are you sure, Mel?"

Melissa swallowed. Lex could see that her eyes were red-rimmed from crying. "No. I'm not," she said quietly. "I don't know if I'm going toward something or just getting away. But it feels right."

She mustered a tiny smile. Then she hugged each of the remaining members of the group. After she'd hugged Lex, she backed up and looked at them.

"We'll walk along the shore as long as we can," Abby said, pointing west. "If there's any sign of civilization, we'll find it. Then we'll just keep going until we hook around and reach the mountain."

"Okay, okay, enough talk," Eric said. "Let's roll."

Abby immediately set out down the beach, not even pausing to speak—or even look back. Eric tipped his hat at the group. Melissa gave everyone a sad smile and began walking, too.

Jackson waited until the others had gone a few yards, then turned and said, "We're together, we'll be fine . . ." He hesitated. ". . . and so will you."

Daley gave him a small wave.

"See ya soon," Jackson said. "If not, see ya later."

Then he, too, turned and began walking up the beach.

Lex, Daley, Taylor, and Nathan watched their

friends silently as they grew smaller and smaller and smaller, heading up the beach.

After a while, Eric turned and yelled something. He was so far away that Lex could barely make it out.

"What'd he say?" Nathan asked, frowning.

Lex looked at the others. They all looked puzzled. Apparently he was thé only one who'd been able to hear what Eric said.

Lex smiled. "I think he said, 'This ain't over yet!' "

**Read all of the books in this action-packed series!**

# #1 Static

Flight 29 DWN has gone down, crash landed, and seven of its survivors—Daley, Nathan, Melissa, Taylor, Lex, Eric, and Jackson—have no idea where they are. They don't know if rescue is coming, or if or when their pilot and his makeshift search party will ever return. They were on their way to a school-sponsored eco-tour when the plane's engine gave out, and they're lucky to even be alive. But with food, water, and shelter being scarce, they're going to have to learn to put their differences aside and work together—before their luck runs out . . .

# #2 The Seven

The stranded passengers of Flight 29 DWN have managed to survive for several days on a deserted tropical island—but they're beginning to wonder if they'll ever be rescued. Luckily, the castaways have honed their survival skills, and they're finding food to eat—however unappetizing it may be. But when personalities clash, fights ensue, and some serious crushes emerge, things *really* start to get interesting. Will the seven be able to stick together to make it until rescue comes—if it ever does?

# #3 The Return

It's been a week since Flight 29 DWN crash-landed on a deserted island. Despite the occasional disagreement, the seven survivors are finally getting into a routine—until they discover that they are not alone. Will this mystery guest be the answer to all of their problems—or a disruption to the balance they've worked so hard to find?

# #4 The Storm

The seven survivors of Flight 29 DWN have learned to trust each other for survival. But one of the passengers has a dark secret. And when all of their video diaries go missing, that secret may be unleashed, with drastic consequences . . .

# #5 Scratch

A storm has destroyed the camp—the food supply has been flooded, many tools are lost, and the boys' tent is in shreds. Jackson and his motley crew are going to have to start from scratch. But there's mutiny afoot as the group splinters off and teamwork dissolves. It's up to Jackson to keep everyone together—but can he handle the pressure?

# Prequel Ten Rules

Before the passengers of Flight 29 DWN ended up on a deserted island, they were surviving a different disaster—high school. Daley and Nathan are neck and neck in an election gone sour, but when nasty campaign posters about Daley are plastered all over school, all eyes are on Nathan. Can Nathan clear his name before the votes are in? And if Nathan isn't guilty, who is? Could Jackson, the mysterious new student, be at the heart of the trouble?

# #6 On Fire

When Eric breaks the camp lighter and the fire goes out, the castaways are in real trouble. That fire is their source of heat, smoke signals, and, most importantly, clean water. No one is having much luck getting the fire going, but when Jackson falls ill from drinking unsanitized water, the heat is really on. Can they get the fire lit again before it's too late for one of their own?